Intercity
Illusions

Dawn Vogel

CONTENTS

To Make Haste   Pg 1

Brick-Red Love   Pg 11

Secret Gladiolus   Pg 15

A Burrito is Not a Sandwich   Pg 17

I Believe   Pg 21

Radiance and Obscurity   Pg 25

Blind Tasting   Pg 27

The Gift   Pg 31

The Owls Are Gonna Get You   Pg 37

Kinuyo-yo   Pg 41

Yokai Hunters   Pg 45

Maija Spencer, Internet Witch   Pg 53

He Who is in the Place of Embalming   Pg 55

Despite All My Rage   Pg 57

The Adversary (Two Stilted Crowns)   Pg 59

One, Two, Three, FOUR!   Pg 61

Fire Bad   Pg 69

Motes and Morsels   Pg 71

Full Weekend Pass   Pg 73

Memorandum from the Panel for the Identification of   Pg 85
Consequentially Chosen Youth

Safe Haven   Pg 87

Hashtag TPE   Pg 91

About the Author   Pg 101

To Make Haste

The photocopier in the rare books area was churning. It was an old machine, but it wasn't usually loud enough for Monique to hear over her music. She pulled out one earbud to listen to the weird rhythm, but before she had a sense of it, the door behind her opened.

"What are you doing to the copier?" Benji, the overnight library supervisor, asked.

"Professor Valenzuela's scan order," Monique said with a shrug. "Never heard it make this noise before."

Benji sighed. "I'll call the service."

"No point," Monique said, not letting the conversation throw her off her groove of scanning. "It's still working, and the preview images look clean. Anyway, the repair service isn't open this time of night, so you'd just be leaving them a message that maybe something's acting up?"

The churning sound shifted to a low thrumming, and the soles of Monique's shoes vibrated even through the anti-fatigue mat.

"Also, you need to check the actual images, not just the previews. How many times do I have to tell you that?"

Roughly three times a night for the past four months. "I'll check 'em when I finish this book. Like I always do. The procedures manual—"

"The procedures manual needs to be updated, especially for night crew staff who work with minimal supervision. Never mind, I'll check them myself." The door slammed as Benji stomped off.

Monique saved her current batch of images and took a deep breath. She'd requested night shift scanning in order to not have to deal with people. In return, the universe had given her Benji, the most uptight control freak she'd ever met. Technically, he was supposed to be running the few library services that stayed active overnight, while she worked on filling copy and scan orders. But since her first day, he'd been checking up on her work, and that he hadn't found any deficiencies seemed to make him even more devoted to making her life a living hell.

It wasn't a hard job. Read the request slips, fill the requests. Make sure the images are legible, which was the whole reason why the library had shelled out the big bucks for a combo copier/scanner with a preview function to show the scans as they were made. Checking them on the computer was for quality assurance.

Monique finished scanning the book and saved her work again. She turned to put it back into the storage cabinet, beside the other books Professor Valenzuela wanted scanned in their entirety.

Books wasn't the right word for them. Tomes was more accurate. Bound in leather, edged in gilt, they were the epitome of rare books. Half of them weighed at least twenty pounds, and Monique wasn't looking forward to hefting those, ever so carefully, hands encased in white cloth gloves, and holding them gingerly on the scanner.

"Eenie meenie minie moe," she muttered under her breath as she selected another book. She slipped her earbud back in, checked the request slip, and started scanning.

She'd gotten halfway through the new book before Benji shouted her name.

She pulled out her earbuds again before turning to face him. "Yes?"

"You're scanning too fast."

"What?"

"The computer. There are five files popping up per minute, and it's doing the spinny death wheel thing. You're not supposed to save each image separately."

"I'm not," Monique said. "And the 'spinny death wheel' means it's processing. I'm sorry that gets in the way of your internet surfing."

Benji frowned, an expression that made him look both angry and disappointed at the same time. "Well, you need to slow down, then."

"Are you sure someone's not transferring files to the computer? I'm working my usual pace, same as always." Monique held up her earbuds. "Keeping in time with the music."

"Well maybe you should go with something a little less dance club appropriate," he said.

Monique pursed her lips. "So, no Tchaikovsky?" She held up her earbuds, from which the faint sounds of classical music played.

"Just follow the manual, okay? Slow down, save often, check your scans. It's not that hard." He stomped back out of the copier room, slamming the door again.

Pausing to stretch her wrists, Monique let her unfocused gaze wander the room. The calendar hadn't been turned to a new month since August, so she took a moment to update it. Flipping to October, she laughed. *Full moon and Friday the thirteenth at midnight. No wonder he's so wound up.*

And no wonder Professor Spooky wants her weird scans emailed before the library opens. Monique returned to her scanning, pausing to glance over the unintelligible language she'd been scanning all evening.

For a moment, the words on the page wavered before her eyes. It didn't last more than a second or two, but she would have sworn the page said "to make haste."

"Yeah, that's just wishful thinking," she murmured under her breath.

The churn of the scanner redoubled, faster and louder than before. Monique didn't even bother with her earbuds as she continued scanning the book, certain Benji would be poking his head back into her business any minute now.

When she finished, she checked the time on her phone. *Time to get away from the copier for a few minutes.* She opened the storage cabinet to put away the last book and stared.

Inside the storage cabinet, the books that had been standing up in neat rows now lay flat on their backs, pages flipping and an eerie blue-white light dancing across their surfaces.

Monique looked around the room and closed the cabinet. She opened it more slowly this time, but the books were still in motion. "That can't be real," she muttered. "Can't be." She walked over to open the door and lean out. "Benji?"

He glanced up at the clock before he answered. "Yeah, you can go on break."

"Um, thanks, but I need you to see something in here."

"Show me after your break, then." He tapped his bare wrist. "Time's wasting. I already clocked you out."

Monique nodded stiffly, grabbing her lunch bag from under the counter and marching outside. The library staff room was always empty at night, but she preferred taking her lunch outside. Especially when possessed books had been moving around in the storage cabinet.

~

Food and fresh air convinced Monique that low blood sugar and too much staring at the scanner LEDs had made the books look like they were animated. She dropped off her lunch bag, stared pointedly at Benji until he clocked her back in, and went into the copier room.

It wasn't better.

The storage cabinet doors stood wide open. Monique was sure she had closed them. Some of the books hovered outside the cabinet, while new books had joined in the page flipping, light-up dance.

"Benji?" she croaked out, barely louder than a whisper.

"What now? I clocked you in."

She shook her head and pointed toward the cabinet.

"Oh, right, what did you want to show me?"

Benji joined Monique in the doorway to the copier room. A faint "huh" escaped his lips as he fainted.

Monique stared at Benji's unmoving body for at least minute. She reached for the desk phone but didn't pick it up. She could call campus security to get Benji an ambulance, but she wasn't sure he needed one. And she had no idea how to explain why he'd fainted.

Instead, she moved the tall chairs away from the desk and rolled Benji toward it, positioning him on his side, in case he threw up. Then she looked back into the copier room. Nothing had changed. She closed the door firmly behind her and looked at the computer where Benji had been checking her scans. Files were still flying into the folder.

A few clicks later, she verified that somehow, the books that were flapping around the copier room were transmitting their pages to the scanned document folder. A chill ran down her spine as she flipped through the scans. But everything was showing up in the order it needed to, and the work was now progressing at ten times her normal speed.

A voice broke her from her reverie. "Problem?"

The young woman standing at the desk wore her multi-colored hair in braids of varying thicknesses and looked as though she had taken about as much care in braiding her hair as she had in choosing her mismatched clothing. For a moment, Monique pegged her as one of the hippie contingent on campus, but the lack of overpowering patchouli quashed that thought.

"No, no problem. Can I help you with anything?"

"Name's Lil."

Monique gestured to her nametag with a stiff smile. "Can I help you with anything, Lil?"

"No. Probably not. Wait, no, yes. This is definitely the weird thing I noticed."

"Sorry?"

Lil smiled broadly. "Strange magical energies are gathering near you, Monique. Really, really strange."

Monique forced a chuckle. "Yeah, I don't believe in magic." *The self-scanning books notwithstanding.*

"You should," Lil replied. She pointed at the copier room door. "It's back there."

"Sorry, library staff only behind the desk," Monique said, moving to intercept Lil.

Lil stopped, but her gaze swung down to Benji's sneakers. "Ooh, was he non-library staff who tried to do something about it? Are you going to smite me?"

"Um, no. He ... he's taking a nap. Night shift, you know. We have to get our sleep when we can."

"Sure." Lil peered at Benji. "Oh, I know him. He's the library police. Don't do this, don't do that."

"Yeah, that sounds like him."

"He doesn't nap on the job."

Monique's shoulders slumped. "No, he doesn't." She took a deep breath, barely believing that she was about to ask her next question. "Okay, let's say there might be something magical in the world—"

"There is," Lil said.

"Then what are you planning to do?"

Lil shrugged. "I just wanted to see what's up." She narrowed her eyes at Monique. "Are you a witch? Is this your doing? Lil isn't my true name. It's a nickname. So don't plan on doing any magic on me, got it?"

"Not a witch," Monique said. "But it might be my doing."

"What did you do?" Lil wrinkled her nose and sniffed the air. "Smells like—" She sneezed loudly. "Ugh, I hate having to smell for magic. I think I'm allergic to half of the things it smells like."

Monique let out a long sigh. She glanced at Benji, but he was still out cold. With one finger over her lips, she beckoned Lil closer.

"Behind the desk?" Lil's eyes grew wide. "Woo hoo, I get to circumvent the library police!"

"Shhh," Monique said. "You don't want to wake him."

"Right." Lil tiptoed behind the desk, exaggerating her movements. "Okay, quiet as a mouse."

Monique gave Lil a tight-lipped smile and opened the copier room door.

"Oh. Whoa. That's ... This is the neatest copier room I've ever seen!"

"Neat like awesome or neat like tidy?" Monique asked, gaze running over the haphazard stacks of books and papers.

"You have a magical copier room," Lil said.

"Sure."

"Only it wasn't magical before tonight—oh, I get it, you did something, and now it's magical. Cool, what did you do?"

"I don't know." Monique paused as she tried to recall what happened. "I thought I saw something in one of the books about haste, and I wished for it, but—"

"Oh! Unbridled wish! Oh crap!" Lil began spinning frantically outside of the copier room.

"'Unbridled?' What does that mean?"

"You unleashed a spell out of one of the books, and it made your wish real. The problem is wishes are tricky. How much thought did you put into it?"

"Um, none, I guess," Monique replied.

Lil beckoned Monique toward her. As Monique stepped out of the copier room, Lil whispered. "Close the door. You don't want the books to hear you right now."

6

Monique did as Lil requested, though she was beginning to wonder why she was listening to Lil at all.

"Okay. You have to unwish your wish. Only you have to really think about it this time. No more unbridled wishes."

"Like what, I want this to stop?"

"No, no way, that's way too vague. You got fast copying because you wished for haste. You got lucky that the wish didn't make you super fast or something. So don't wish for slowness, either, because you might turn into a turtle, like my Great-Aunt Hilda."

Monique wanted to ask if Hilda had always been a turtle or turned into one, but she wasn't sure she wanted to lead Lil down that path. "Okay. Should I tell you my wish?"

"No! Wait, maybe." Lil frowned and exhaled forcefully. "I don't know. You shouldn't do it on your own, but if you tell me, it might not come true. Like birthday candle wishes. Think about what you're going to wish for and if there's any possible way it could be misinterpreted. And then, when you're really sure, go back in the copier room and, you know, wish."

"Okay, I'll give it a shot."

Lil smiled broadly. "Cheers, then. I'll sneak back out before the library police wakes up."

Before Monique could ask Lil anything else, the other young woman scurried out from behind the desk and vanished around the nearest corner.

"That was thoroughly unhelpful," Monique muttered under her breath as she stepped back into the copier room. Glancing over her shoulder to be sure that Lil was gone, she closed the door.

Books continued to flap around the space, but Monique dodged past them to get to the copier. On a whim, she pushed the Clear button.

Something screeched, and Monique wondered if everything was about to come crashing down around her. She covered her head and tucked her chin down, but the flapping sounds only got louder. The pages were fluttering faster when she peeked out from between her arms.

Nothing was on the scanner glass, so the Clear button shouldn't have had an impact, logically. All of the duplication was taking place in the air now. Despite that, Monique fumbled for the copier's power switch. Clouds of dust (she hoped) began puffing out of some of the books.

Monique still had her wish in mind, but she had one more thing to try. She scooted behind the copier and unplugged it from the wall. But still the books hung above and around her, pages turning faster and faster, and more dust, now mixed with fragments of aged leather, fell from the books. This had to stop if the rare books were to remain intact.

Taking a deep breath, she spoke her wish aloud. "I wish everything would go back to normal."

~

Monique wasn't sure how long she'd been standing at the copier when the door opened behind her.

"How much more of Professor Valenzuela's scan order is left?" Benji asked.

Monique glanced over at the cabinet. "Two more books."

Benji sighed loudly. "You've got half an hour left on your shift. If you don't get it done—"

"It'll be done."

"Good. You've had all night to work on it."

"Yep," Monique said. "Been working on it all night. How do the images look?"

"Fine, I guess. I don't read Latin or whatever these books are in."

"Yeah, me either." Monique closed the book she was working on and considered asking Benji if he was alright. But he hadn't said anything about passing out, so maybe he had forgotten about seeing the floating books. She could keep that bit to herself. Knowing that he'd fainted in the face of magic, even if he didn't acknowledge it, might make working with him a little easier. "One more left. I should get to it."

"Right. Carry on."

"Thanks, Benji. Glad we made it through another night of thrilling scanning."

"Yeah, whatever."

There we go. Everything back to how it was. But Monique made a note of the call number for the book she had wished on. Never a bad thing to know how to make haste.

———

Originally published by *The Overcast*, February 2018.

Brick-Red Love

Today was supposed to be the happiest day in Tanith's life—her wedding day. But it was still three hours to the wedding, and Tanith had already had her fill of the chaos. She slipped out of the dressing room while everyone else oohed and ahhed and giggled and squealed over how beautiful Vicki's hair was, studded with several dozen rhinestones. They'd glimmer even through her veil.

Most brides selected their home church for their wedding, but Tanith hadn't been home in years. Vicki didn't have a home church either, so they'd settled on this little non-denominational chapel in the middle of the woods. Tanith headed for a small clearing she and Vicki had found behind the church when they first visited. It was tranquil outside, still an hour or more before the first guests would be arriving. She could get a few minutes of peace and then head back in for the final touches on her dress, makeup, and hair.

The last thing she expected to see in the clearing was a door.

Her breath caught in her throat. This was not just any door. It was the door to her parent's house, halfway across the country. There was no mistaking the bold brick-red paint, nor the carved doorjamb that surrounded it. She ran her fingers over the wood, finding the places where she and her siblings had defaced the doorjamb in the subtlest of ways—adding an extra line here, a hole there, leaving their mark on the family home.

She was still touching the doorjamb when the door flew open, her father standing within. "What are you doing, Tanith? Come in from the cold."

It wasn't cold where she was standing, but her father was bundled up in a sweater and wool slacks. It would be cold where he was. But how could he be here, or she be there?

11

Tanith glanced back toward the chapel, then looked at her father. "How?"

He shrugged. "Haven't a clue. Don't look a gift horse in the mouth. Come in and say hello to everyone."

She peered past her father. Pots and pans clanged in the kitchen; her mother was an apparition in the cloud of steam hovering at the kitchen door. Some of her nieces and nephews played a card game on the living room floor. Her brother Davis had fallen asleep stretched out on the couch, while her sister-in-law, Nora, knitted nearby. The others were probably in the backyard, in spite of the cold.

The aroma of chili wafted over her, and her mouth watered. One of her nieces—April, Tanith thought, though she'd only seen the girl in photos—waved her cards in Tanith's direction.

Home, with the smells and the memories. Her heart ached. She wanted to share it with the woman who'd won her heart.

"Let me go get Vicki."

"No time." Her father grabbed her by the wrist, gripping it tight.

Tanith jerked away. "No, she should come too. I mean, we're getting married today. She's part of the family."

Her father crossed his arms over his chest, and Tanith shuddered. This was too unreal, and yet too real. Her father managed to express his disapproval across time and space, his glare making her feel ten years old again, when he had lectured her that kissing other girls wasn't what nice young ladies did.

"You don't want to see her. You just want to pull me away," Tanith said, shaking her head. "Figures."

"We just want you to come home, Tanith."

Tanith took a deep breath. She'd endure the chaos of the wedding preparation to not be here right now. "Too bad. I don't want to come home." She took a step backward. "Tell the family I said hello, if you would. I miss them."

"And me?" her father asked.

Tanith shrugged. "A little bit. But not enough to deny my heart. We hope you'll come around someday."

She didn't give him an opportunity to respond, turning and running back into the dressing room.

Vicki looked up when Tanith entered. "Where've you been, love?"

Tanith leaned down and kissed Vicki's shoulder where it met her neck, avoiding the makeup and hairspray. "I thought I needed some fresh air. Didn't help, though. Maybe some water, instead."

Vicki caught Tanith's hand and kissed it, leaving a brick-red lipstick print there, the same color as the door to Tanith's childhood home. "Somebody got a pair of earbuds Tanith can use?" She smiled at Tanith. "Marge can work her magic while you relax."

Tanith smiled back and clutched the hand with the lipstick print to her heart. It might look ridiculous in the wedding photos, but she wasn't going to let anyone clean it off her hand.

It was all the love she needed.

Originally published in *The Arcanist*, April 2019.

Secret Gladiolus

Eight flowers stitched into my skin,
gladiolus, blooming eternally.
We joked about them being for when
I haven't another stitch to wear.

The memory of the sting and burn
of the machine, pulling, poking,
embedding the ink, my blood as red
as their petals, as you looked on.

Two years later, you were gone.
Two years later, I had changed.
From such pain comes beauty,
and something unexpected too.

The flowers burst forth,
their petals emerge from my flesh.
I have bouquets every morning,
leaving wilted stems every evening.

But only for August, the month of the gladiolus,
then hidden within my skin the rest of the year.
Unknown by all those who see my ink,
and a secret you'll never learn.

Originally published in *WLYA 2019 Anthology*, December 2019.

A Burrito is Not a Sandwich

Amanda was running late for her first appointment of the morning, thanks to the line at the coffee shop. Since the wall between the worlds had fallen and destroyed the kingdoms on the other side, the city's population had swelled, putting a strain on businesses. Most people had accepted it as the new normal, but they had not completely adjusted to this new way.

"Your 8:30 is in your office," her assistant said as Amanda hurried through the lobby.

"Thanks, Becky. Loan application?"

Becky nodded. "Displaced fae."

Amanda's lips pressed together. Loan applications from displaced peoples from the other world were more complicated than standard loan applications. But the displaced peoples deserved to make a living just as anyone else did, so the bank had done what they could to introduce revised processes. She'd have to focus on their business plan, and, as her boss always reminded her, think outside the proverbial box.

Gauging ages of the fae was difficult, but the two seated in Amanda's office appeared to be an adult and an adolescent. The elder of the two was tall and willowy, skin tinted violet, dressed in a long quilted robe that might look like a dressing gown on an elderly human, but looked more ceremonial in this setting. The younger fae was broader in the face, their skin a faint shade of russet, and wore jeans and sneakers, but their shirt shifted in texture and color as Amanda circled her desk to sit behind it. She suspected it wasn't just a trick of the light, but inherent magic in the fabric.

"Apologies for my delay," she said as she sat. "My name is Amanda. Why don't you tell me a little about yourselves and your plan while I load your application?"

The elder fae spoke. "I am Sen. This is my business partner, Aoi. He is, as you say, the brains behind the operation."

Amanda expected Aoi to launch into a pitch for the business at this point, but he remained silent. She logged into her computer, and still had received no additional information from the pair. "Could you tell me about your plan?"

"Gelato burrito," Aoi said, his voice gravelly and deeper than Amanda expected.

"I ... what?"

"Gelato burrito," Aoi repeated.

"I understand the words you're saying, but not how they go together," Amanda admitted.

Aoi produced a white paper wrapped bundle and placed it on Amanda's desk. It was roughly eight inches long and three inches in diameter, and cold vapor roiled from it. Unwrapping the bundle, Aoi revealed what appeared to be a soft waffle cone wrapped like a tortilla. He then unwrapped the tortilla, revealing neat layers of color, one studded with blackberries, another with small chunks of mango, a third with black specks Amanda hoped were ground vanilla beans.

"Huh." Amanda paused. "Nope, I still don't get it."

"It is a burrito containing gelato, as a dessert treat," Sen said.

"Okay, like a peanut ice cream roll? From Taiwan?"

Sen and Aoi exchanged glances before Sen replied. "The principle may be the same, but the gelato burrito is purely sweet, without a savory element like the peanut ice cream roll."

Amanda realized she might need to ask different questions to get the responses she needed to understand the business plan. "Fair enough. So you want to start a dessert restaurant?"

Sen and Aoi nodded in unison.

"And will the gelato burrito be the sole offering?"

"We understand that there are a number of gelato-based locales here in the city, so we wanted to approach the subject matter differently," Sen replied. "If customers wished, they could have their gelato without the wrapping, but what would be the point?"

Aoi spoke up, finally saying more than two words. "It's a variation on an ice cream sandwich honoring the cultural contributions of the Italian and Mexican peoples."

"A burrito is not a sandwich," Amanda said, a frown springing to her lips as she recalled the number of times she had debated this exact topic with friends and family.

"I never said it was," Aoi replied.

Amanda glared at her computer monitor, willing the loan application to load so she could redirect the conversation, which was going sideways. A gelato burrito restaurant wasn't much of a business plan. It was an idea, and a weird one at that.

She took a deep breath. Think outside the box, she reminded herself. "Is the tort ... cone ... outside soft or hard?"

"Both," Sen and Aoi replied in unison.

"Try it," Sen urged.

"I can't," Amanda blurted out. Her inborn fear of offered food emerged unbidden. There were rules about this. If you ate something offered by the fae, you were trapped in their land forever.

Sen and Aoi's expressions fell, both of them looking down at their laps. Aoi reached toward the burrito, but Sen stayed the younger fae's hand.

"I'm sorry," Amanda said. "That was rude." She took a deep breath. Her fear was irrational, and she knew it. It was unfair as well. These fae just wanted to make their way in a new home. There was no proof that they entrapped humans who ate their food, only old wives' tales. Maybe those stemmed from a fear of the unknown, rules humans had made to keep their children from mixing with other peoples. Rules that could not continue in a society that wanted to be inclusive.

Amanda took several deep breaths to calm herself, trying to form a polite response to salvage this meeting. "Bank policy doesn't allow us to accept gifts from loan applicants." She smiled. "Perhaps if your business gets off the ground, I can visit it and try a gelato burrito then."

Her screen flashed with the opened application, and Amanda turned to the safe, factual data presented there. The application listed their credit history at the First Bank of The Sanctuary (dissolved) and their cash flow history (not converted to local currencies). Frustrated, she scrolled through more pages of information. The collateral offered was a jewelry collection, again tied to The Sanctuary (listed as "priceless" in the valuation), and their character references were other displaced peoples with no permanent Earth addresses listed.

It was, to be blunt, a mess. Had this application come across her desk with no information about the applicants, she would have declined it without even a meeting. Changed times, however, called for a change in methods.

Amanda returned her attention to the gelato burrito sitting on her desk. She could imagine the flavor profile, the sweet and tart flavors of the gelato as they mingled with the shell. If she'd ordered this dessert herself, she'd replace the vanilla layer with sweet cream gelato, but the choices made were sensible from a culinary standpoint.

People would flock to a restaurant serving such an unusual combination. She could picture the restaurant already—bare lightbulbs hanging from the ceiling in clusters, long tables lined with metal stools, tin letters spelling out the name of the shop in lights. It would be a hipster's dream come true. It would thrive here, a city already working to blend human cultures and now integrating displaced peoples from another world.

Amanda returned her attention to the application, looking for a name to complete her mental image of the proposed restaurant. "What are you going to call the place?" she asked.

Aoi hesitated. "Gelato burrito?"

"Alright, we're going to need to do some work on your application, but you've sold me on your concept. Let's make this happen."

I Believe

There's a monster under my bed. Her name is Hermana. She's black and gray striped like a tiger, but she looks more like a teddy bear with fangs and claws.

She doesn't like her name. I told her she could use mine, but she doesn't think Chloe suits her, and it's hard to pronounce with her fangs.

I told her she can call me "E", because that's the easy part of my name.

Hermana-who-does-not-want-to-be-Chloe is best friends with the monster in my closet. Their name is Bug, but they don't look like a bug. They're round in the middle with some spindly limbs. Sometimes three, sometimes seven, and one time, thirty-twelve.

Which isn't a real number, but that's how many there were.

They only have thirty-twelve legs when there's trouble.

The trouble won't come inside, though, because we have other house monsters too. Felix under the stairs, who nips at my toes when I go up and down. Chuckles in the chimney, who laughs or howls, depending on his mood. And Granny in the attic.

Not my real Granny. That's just her name. I hear her rocking chair, soothing me and her, when I go to bed.

Hermana told me about the last incursion. That's a fancy word for attack. The outside monsters tried to come inside, before we moved here.

The last family didn't believe in monsters under the bed, in the closet, under the stairs, up the chimney, or in the attic. And that made the house monsters sad and weak. So they couldn't stop in the incursion of the outside monsters.

I've seen the outside monsters. That's how I know the house monsters are nice. The ones outside have no skin, sharp teeth, big eyes that never blink. And they tell me they like to eat Chloes and Mommies and Daddies.

I told them no.

I believe in my monsters. They promise to keep me safe. They'll keep Mommy and Daddy safe too, as long as I believe.

~

I still believe in monsters, and I'm going to keep on believing.

Mom and Dad think it's just a phase, that I'll grow up someday. But I won't doubt.

The outside monsters go to my school now. They have names like Chet and Tiffany. They pretend they're human, but I see them for what they are. No skin, sharp teeth, big eyes that never blink.

I tell Mom and Dad I want to be homeschooled, but they say no.

I hide in the library a lot and find the books about monsters. The books don't talk about my house monsters, but that's okay. I still believe.

The books do tell me enough to cobble together a plan on how to stop the outside monsters. I only wear silver jewelry. I carry bags of herbs. The outside monsters like Chet and Tiffany call me witch and freak, but I don't listen.

They stay away.

But the house monsters don't like my silver and my herbs either. It makes them uncomfortable too. They're not so different from the outside monsters, they tell me. They've just chosen to be good.

They promise they'll stay in the house, but they have to keep their distance.

No friends at school. No more friends at home.

I still believe.

~

It's hard to believe in monsters once you're in the real world. The people are bad enough. Or maybe the monsters have learned to pretend to be people. They wear fake skins, file their sharp teeth down, and teach themselves to blink.

I'm too busy dealing with people, and I forget about Hermana, Bug, Felix, Chuckles, and Granny.

I don't hear their voices when I call Mom. (Dad left after I did.) She's going to sell the house anyway, because she doesn't need all that space.

And in my cozy apartment in the city, with no more ties to my old house, and dealing with people who are worse than monsters most of the time, I'd forget about my monsters entirely.

If I didn't smell Granny's lavender, hear Chuckles voice, feel Felix nipping at my toes, taste the cotton candy sweet of Bug's round middle, and see Hermana on my doorstep.

"Do you still believe?" they ask.

I'd stopped, just for a moment. And they had to find me.

I do still believe.

There are no stairs or chimney or attic in my cozy apartment, but we make do.

Hermana and Felix share the space under my bed. Chuckles joins Bug in my closet.

Granny doesn't take up space, just rocks the other chair while I watch TV.

I do still believe.

—————

Originally published in *The Future Fire*, May 2019.

Radiance and Obscurity

(A Paradelle)

Your blue eyes dance with (warmth of) stars.
Your blue eyes dance with warmth (of stars);
You cast magic of love from beside me.
You cast magic of love. From beside me,
Love, your eyes, you of warmth, from dance cast of blue,
Beside me, with magic stars.

We'll have been out, and I dress in light.
We'll have been out, and I dress. In light,
And there's you, in my midnight dark gown.
And there's you (in my midnight dark gown).
There's my gown and I in midnight light
We'll have you dress dark, been in and out.

Now in our brightest we stalk, altogether.
Now in our brightest (we stalk) altogether.
The chandeliers—among the twinkling—
The chandeliers, among the twinkling.
Now we in our altogether stalk among
The brightest, the twinkling chandeliers.

Now there's dark magic in our eyes.
We have been cast out from the brightest light.
Altogether, love, you and I stalk warmth,
With you in your dress of twinkling stars,
Beside me in my gown of midnight blue,
And we'll dance among the chandeliers

Originally published in *Liquid Imagination*, November 2019.

Blind Tasting

Hollis wasn't sure why she'd agreed to let Macy set her up on a blind date, but here she was, heading down the stairs to a tiny, hole-in-the-wall bar. She checked her phone to see if she had any messages from Macy or Macy's friend ... what was the name Macy had given? Charlie?

It was quarter to seven, and the date was set for seven-thirty, but Hollis was always early. At least on this occasion, it meant she'd have time to have a glass of wine to smooth out the fluttering in her stomach.

The bar was even tinier than it had looked from the outside—a low ceiling, half a dozen bar stools, and an equal number of intimate round tables, two chairs apiece, lit by flickering tea lights in cut glass holders. The bar itself had slightly better lighting, but it was enough for Hollis to see the bartender was the only other person there.

The bartender gave Hollis a coy smile, her midnight black hair whispering across her shoulders as she leaned forward. "What'll it be?"

Hollis glanced behind the bartender, trying to spot a bottle of wine she could order with confidence. Failing that, she searched for a hand-written menu on any of the walls near the bar. Still nothing she could work with. She shrugged. "What do you have that's red and smooth?"

The bartender leaned an elbow on the bartop, thinking, then smiled. Hollis's stomach flip-flopped at the smile. Maybe if this blind date didn't pan out, she could chat up the bartender instead. "I've got just the thing." The bartender ducked behind the bar and produced a dark unlabeled and unopened bottle and a stemless wine glass.

Hollis spun in her seat and looked around the bar while the bartender opened the bottle. "Is it usually this quiet on a Monday night?"

"Most Mondays, yes," the bartender said, pulling the cork free with a pop.

Hollis intended to request just a taste of this unidentified wine. But as the contents flowed from the bottle into her glass, she was entranced. The wine was vivid indigo, not the crimson she expected. In the dim light of the bar, a touch of effervescence made it look like it was glittering with stardust. "What the—?"

The bartender tilted her head and half-shrugged. "Try it."

Hollis took a deep breath, reminding herself the bottle had been sealed. The wine's appearance had to be a trick of the dim lighting, nothing sinister. It was the only thing that made sense.

Macy had sent her on this blind date because she thought Hollis needed to be open to more possibilities. She didn't want to prove Macy right. She had to try the wine.

She swirled the wine in the glass and sniffed it. Aside from a faint aroma of blueberries, which weren't out of place for a red, the wine smelled normal enough.

She took a tentative sip. The flavor exploded on her palate, but it was perfectly balanced and smooth. Giving the first sip a moment to settle, she took a second sip, marveling at how much better the wine already tasted, even without an opportunity to breathe.

The two sips had also made the bar seem brighter, giving Hollis a better look at the bartender. The woman's eyes were the same color as the wine, indigo, dappled with stars. Hollis had never seen anything like those eyes. She was smitten.

Breathlessly, Hollis said, "I like it. Now will you tell me what it is?"

The bartender grinned, again loosing the butterflies in Hollis's stomach. "Blind date wine."

"Is it that obvious?" Hollis asked, her shoulders sagging.

"Only because Macy sent me a photo."

Hollis hesitated before taking another sip, realizing what was going on. "You're Charlie?"

The bartender nodded. "Sorry I didn't introduce myself right away."

"That's alright," Hollis said quickly. "I just didn't realize she was sending me on a date with the bartender at the bar where we were meeting."

"Owner," Charlie said. "It's quiet on Mondays because I'm normally closed. But it's a good icebreaker for a blind date." She grinned. "Now that we're both on the same page, I can whip up some heavy appetizers, or we can go somewhere else for dinner. Your choice."

Hollis took another sip of wine. Even without the wine and Charlie's unearthly eyes, she was still intrigued. Maybe this wouldn't be a bad date after all. "Does somewhere else have this same wine?" she asked.

Charlie shook her head. "No, that one's pretty exclusive to my bar. At least around here."

Hollis smiled. "Then pour yourself a glass, let me give you a hand in the kitchen, and you can tell me where this wine, and you, came from."

Originally published in *Every Day Fiction*, March 2021.

The Gift

T'was the night before Christmas, and I wasn't done with my shopping. There was only one person I wanted to buy a gift. I knew she'd understand if I didn't give her anything, but I wanted to. I needed to see her eyes sparkle with delight.

I worked until close, which meant there were no shops open by the time I was done.

Well, no shops above ground.

I'd heard rumors about the Goblin Market. Mostly whispers filled with regrets, but other murmurs suggested there might be something worth finding. Something that wouldn't come at too dear of a price.

Working in retail, I talked to a lot of people. Enough of them had given me directions to the Goblin Market. Some of them were contradictory. I'd teased out the pieces that weren't, and I was pretty sure I had the route figured out.

Half a block down Main, take the alley through to First, and then use the half-alley to get to the courtyard in the back of the Highland Apartments building. Turn around three times widdershins (which I had to look up—counterclockwise, it turns out), back the way you came, and the entryway would reveal itself.

I was a little leery of that last detail. Reveal itself how? I guessed I'd have to just try it.

I didn't see a soul on the streets as I made my way to Main. The alleys were empty too, bearing the lingering scent of garbage. A sleek black cat sat on the fountain in the Highland Apartments courtyard, cleaning itself. It looked at me, blinked its big green eyes, and resumed ignoring me, even as I turned three times.

The half-alley felt different when I stepped back into it. Cleaner, less smelly. And brighter, even though there were no more lights

31

than there had been before. When I reached the other alley, people strolled down it. People who weren't dressed for the winter weather.

A bead of sweat rolled down my cheek, my hat, scarf, gloves, and heavy coat now too much for the temperature. As I shucked them all, more people passed me, shouting out greetings to one another.

A wave of panic passed over me. Would I be allowed to shop in a place I had never been before? Was this a secret club I was violating?

More importantly, now that I was on my way, could I even change my mind?

I had no choice but to follow the crowd. At least I didn't have to worry about the entrance being revealed. They'd lead me to it.

There wasn't a door on the side of the old brick building before, but that's where they were headed. A riot of smells, sounds, and colored lights poured from the doorway, coming from somewhere down the stairs.

Folks filled in behind me, giving me no choice but to continue into the belly of the beast, as it were.

I reached the bottom of the stairs and realized I'd dropped one of my gloves. I turned to see if I could spot it, but the steady stream of people descending prevented me from going back. Clearly, this was the entrance. I hoped I'd find an exit.

Then I turned to take in the sights, and I knew I was in the right place.

The booths were bedecked with curtains, streamers, and more twinkle lights than I'd ever seen, giving the whole place an ethereal feeling. The aromas were earthy but spiced with otherworldly scents. There were snippets of conversation I couldn't follow, and others I could, and music from throats and instruments unlike anything of the waking world. I wanted to take pictures, or video, but I felt like that would be a violation of the inherent secrecy here.

I let the wave of shoppers carry me along past the vendors, catching the barest glimpses of their wares. Every table was a mix of simple practical items and tantalizing slivers of something special, magical. I was glad I wasn't ready to shop yet, because I couldn't have stopped to look at anything I was interested in, as the crowd swept me along.

And then, before I knew it, I was back out on the street, the cold air nipping at my bare fingers and face. The swirls of lights and colors and scents already felt like nothing more than a dream.

I had to get back. I ran, ignoring the cold, to the place where I started. The door that had appeared was gone now, so I followed the directions again.

Half a block down Main, alley through to First, half-alley to the courtyard behind the Highland Apartments building.

I breathed a sigh of relief when I rejoined the stream of shoppers headed to the Goblin Market. This time, I reminded myself, I'd step out of the flow of traffic and shop.

My other glove was gone by the time I reached the bottom of the stairs. I had no idea if I'd lost it during my first pass through the Market, on my mad sprint back, or on my second trip down the stairs. Wherever it was, it wasn't important. I could replace a pair of gloves. I was back inside, and I wasn't going to wander out again without getting what I came for.

The throng of humanity moving through the main thoroughfare was less pressing now, but as long as I was within that mass of people, I wouldn't have the opportunity to shop. Instead of looking at the wares, I scanned the pathway ahead, identifying a dark hallway to the left near the midpoint of the Market. That was where I could step out of the flow and work my way along the booths, swimming upstream, as it were, to find a gift.

The hallway was narrower than I anticipated, barely wide enough to squeeze through sideways, like some of the shelving in the stockroom at work. At the opposite end was more light, more smells, and fewer shoppers. I hadn't seen this part of the Goblin Market on my first pass. Maybe there would be something better in this other section. I grinned and picked up my side-shuffling pace.

My scarf slid out of my hands like someone had yanked on one end, and I looked back the direction I'd come. The opposite end of my scarf was caught on a nail or splinter at the end of this passageway, and before I could chase after the end nearest me, a hand snatched the snagged end and pulled the entire scarf out of my sight.

I sighed. It wasn't dear to me. Just an old scarf I'd worn for years. It, like my gloves, could be replaced.

I reached the end of the hallway, which opened into another section of the Goblin Market. In this space, though, I could see the wares and their vendors. I could walk up to any table I liked and peruse the offerings.

Finally, I could find a gift.

The first table I passed was covered in shoes, all of them without a match, most of which had seen better days.

"Interested in a trade?" the vendor asked, eyeing my boots.

"No thanks," I replied. "I need these."

The next table was covered with paper flowers—cute, but not quite what I wanted. The woman selling them worked on another while she followed me with her gaze, never once looking down to make sure she'd folded the paper correctly.

I passed by three or four more tables, none of them bearing anything that caught my eye. I wondered if this space was for the vendors who didn't have the sort of flashy items the front space held. I thought about going back, braving the crowd, and finding something there to take home.

A door slammed open nearby, bringing with it a blast of icy cold, reminding me too much of my previous accidental exit from the Goblin Market. I wouldn't try to go back to the main room. I'd have to make do with something here.

A young girl stumbled through the open door and closed it, blocking the wind. She wore a thin shirt and slacks, nowhere close to sufficient for the weather.

I frowned, looking around to see if any of the vendors were paying attention to this girl. She had to be the daughter of one of them. But no one looked in her direction.

"Are you alright?" I asked.

She started at my words, a confused expression crossing her face. "Pardon?" she murmured.

I pointed toward the door. "It's cold out there. Aren't you freezing?"

"Yes, but there's nothing for it."

Her statement was matter of fact, but it hit me all the same. I could do something about her being cold. I'd lost my gloves and scarf, but I still had my hat—the one I'd worn for years, still warm. Without even thinking, I held it out to her. "Here. You need this more than me."

A smile crept across her face as she reached for the hat. "Thank you." She pulled it down over her hair, covering her ears and nearly covering her eyes. Her smile remained, bright and beaming.

"Let me do you a favor, now." She looked around, then tapped twice on the door she'd come through. Stepping to the other side, she opened the door, using a handle that had appeared where the hinges had been.

I blinked at the improbability of it, but when she stepped out of the doorway, the space beyond was red and golden, with a palpable warmth radiating out, even at a dozen feet from the room, where I stood.

"You'll find what you need inside," she said.

Drifting forward, I barely felt the rough cement beneath my feet. The room drew me toward it with promises of exactly what I was looking for.

Beyond the door stood a young boy who could have been the girl's twin, or definitely a sibling. He held his arms out, palms up, like a doorman or porter at a fine hotel.

Without even thinking, I laid my coat across his arms. I marveled at the colors within—while the entryway was red and golden, a little bit beyond that was a section of blues and greens, silvers and bronzes beyond that, a black and orange section that reminded me of Halloween, and then, finally, an array of violet and rose like the world had never seen.

In the center of that final section sat a tiara, shimmering pink with a dozen faceted stones in as many shades of purple. It was at once beautiful and gaudy, a princess's treasure and a child's toy.

It was perfect.

From nowhere, an old man, dressed in a tuxedo, appeared and lifted the cream and gold satin pillow the tiara rested upon. "Monsieur?" he asked, cocking his head to the side.

"Yes, it's perfect," I breathed, reaching to pick it up. It was the right size and weight, with velvet lining the inside and padding near the ends, so it wouldn't pull hair or pinch.

"Very good," the old man said.

"Wait, how much?" I asked, but the old man was already gone.

So, too, was the boy at the door, and the girl outside.

"My coat?" I asked.

A voice came from deeper within the shop, or perhaps from all around me. "Is an acceptable payment for the item you chose."

And then the scene outside the door was no longer the back space of the Goblin Market, but an alley, and me without gloves, scarf, hat, or coat.

But I still had the tiara.

~

I shivered the whole way home, running to keep myself from freezing solid. I held the tiara tightly enough to ensure I kept my grip on it when my fingers went numb, but gingerly enough to not bend it out of shape.

Mrs. Kellogg, the sitter, was in my recliner, watching something silent on the TV and knitting. "Good gravy, where's your coat?"

"Long story." I didn't want to try to explain where I'd been or what I'd done. Mrs. Kellogg was an honorary part of our family, but she never understood "flights of fancy," as she called everything that didn't fit into her worldview. "Is she sleeping?"

The bedroom door creaked open, a pair of eyes peeking out from the crack.

Even if I wanted to hide the tiara and wrap it, it was too late now. Those eyes lit up like the sun, and she rushed out of her room. "Daddy, is that for me?"

Mrs. Kellogg turned to admonish her but stopped abruptly.

"You bet, Pumpkin. Merry Christmas."

I barely got the tiara on her head before she tackled my legs in an enormous hug.

"You like it?" I asked.

She didn't speak, just looked up at me, her eyes still glowing.

"I'll see you tomorrow," Mrs. Kellogg murmured, letting herself out of the apartment.

I didn't have a spare coat, and I needed to go out for new winter gear sooner rather than later. But in that moment, I didn't care. I'd made my daughter's day.

The look on her face made it all worth it.

Originally published in *The Bronzeville Bee*, December 2019.

The Owls Are Gonna Get You

Momma always told me "The owls are gonna get you, if you don't act right."

Problem was, I was on my best behavior when the owls got me.

Then again, it wasn't like they were boogeyman owls, the kind I had suspected would come after me.

I was in my room, studying, with the window open, because it was hotter than it had any right to be in October. And this owl, bigger than the alley cats that live outside restaurants, landed on my windowsill. Middle of the afternoon. Just blinked and did that weird owl thing where it tilts its head and looks at you sideways.

Then it spoke. "Miss Delaney Brown, I presume?"

I blinked at the owl a few times. "Did you say my name?"

"If you are Miss Delaney Brown, then yes, I did." The owl's mouth moved when it talked, like when TV shows pretend an animal is talking by giving it peanut butter or whatever.

"You're an owl."

"Yes, I am."

"Owls don't talk."

The owl chuckled. "Oh my, you've more to learn than we expected. My fellows call me Professor Agnes. You've been chosen by the parliament to attend the Greater New York Wizarding Academy. The students call it 'Knee-Wah.'"

I was glad I was sitting at my desk as Professor Agnes explained. If I'd been standing up, I would have fallen over. This was some fantasy novel level nonsense. "There's no wizarding academy in New York."

"No? Then where did I come from?"

"I dunno, you're probably a drone or something." I lunged toward the owl, trying to grab her so I could figure out how someone had put this thing together.

Professor Agnes flapped her wings once, powerful enough to launch herself backward off my windowsill and knock me down before I even touched her feathers. "Miss Brown, manners, please."

"I must be dreaming," I muttered, pinching my arm. No luck. Professor Agnes was still there.

"Okay, okay," I said. "Let's say I believe you. What are you gonna tell Momma? She's not gonna let me run off with some owl to some school. Oh, and how much does it cost? Cuz I don't think we can afford a private school unless there's a lot of scholarships."

"Your mother will receive a letter explaining that you've been admitted to the Greater New York Academy for Excellence in Knowledge, all expenses paid." She smiled, which made no sense for an owl to be able to do. "Easy as rain."

"Greater New York ... what do they call that one for short?"

"Kneek. It's a rough approximation combining all the vowels."

"Yeah, okay." I took a deep breath. "Next question. Maybe the one I should have started with. I'm a wizard?"

Professor Agnes chuckled again. "Of course you are, Miss Brown. I wouldn't be here otherwise."

"Of course," I said.

"'Laney?" Momma's voice echoed down the hallway. "You home?"

My gaze ping-ponged between the owl and the door to my room. I might have been making nice with Professor Agnes, but Momma would shoo that owl out of my room the moment she stepped in. "Wait here," I whispered to Professor Agnes, before calling out, "Just a second, Momma!"

I waited until Professor Agnes had returned to the windowsill and got mostly out of sight, and then closed my door before I ran to the living room.

Momma bustled around like she always did, tidying up things that didn't need it. She looked up from the pile of mail on the end table and frowned. "What is that in your hair, Delaney?"

My hands flew to my hair, patting down the cloud of black curls. I couldn't find anything, and my panic edged upward.

Momma plucked something from my hair. An owl feather. "The owls are gonna get you, if you don't act right," she murmured.

That didn't help with my panic. I started sweating. "I wasn't doing anything wrong," I pleaded.

Momma looked past me toward my bedroom.

"I was studying, I swear!"

That regained Momma's attention. "Oh, I know, baby girl."

My brow furrowed as I tried to make sense of what she'd said.

She held the feather between both hands. Only she wasn't holding it—it hovered between her hands, upright, twirling in a breeze that wasn't there.

I blinked. "Momma?"

My bedroom door flew open, like it hadn't been latched shut and a gust of wind had blown through the apartment. The air rushed past me and tingled against my skin.

"Professor Agnes," Momma said, bowing low toward my room.

"Wait, what?" I looked at Professor Agnes, who had flown into the living room, and then back to Momma, who was watching the owl like nothing weird was happening.

"Artemsia, it's good to see you." Professor Agnes landed on the armrest of the sofa.

"'Artemsia'?" I repeated. Momma had always been "Artie" to her friends, but she'd never told me what it stood for.

Momma chuckled and nodded. "Cat's out of the bag, eh?"

Nothing made sense. I raised my hand. "Excuse me, Momma, Professor Agnes, will someone please tell me what's going on?"

"So you've met," Momma said, "and she's told you you're going to wizard school?"

I nodded. "Well, yeah, but she acted like we'd have to keep it a secret from you."

"All part of the ruse, baby girl," Momma said. "What do you think, Professor Agnes?"

Professor Agnes ruffled her feathers, acting like a real owl for once. "Her practicality matches your own, Artemsia. She'll do the Brown family proud."

"That's my baby girl." Momma smiled.

"Congratulations, Delaney," Professor Agnes said. "Welcome to the Greater New York Wizarding Academy."

"That's it, then?" I looked at Momma. "I'm off to wizard school? And with an *owl*, no less?"

Momma chuckled and gave a half-hearted shrug. "I might have fibbed about why the owls were gonna get you, but I told you they would."

Kinuyo-yo

Kinuyo scrambled off the ferry, trying to avoid the usual taunts that followed her.

"Bye, Kinuyo-yo!"

There it was. She'd thought her yo-yo tricks would gain her the respect of her peers. Instead, they'd just given them something else to tease her about. The teachers claimed it was a pun based on her name, but Kinuyo knew what the other students meant by "yo-yo." It wasn't just a pun. They'd identified her as different, and therefore subject to their cruelty.

The ferry stop was flooded, again. The water seeped into her shoes, soaking her socks to her knees. Ever since the Yodo had overtopped its banks and Osaka Bay had surged into the city streets, there hadn't been a moment of dry. The rain hadn't stopped in months.

She threw her yo-yo and snapped it back to her hand, not in the mood for her usual tricks. The damp wasn't good for the string, but the simple rhythm of throw and return kept her calm.

Finally tucking her yo-yo into her pocket, she unfurled her umbrella, for all the good it did. The wind blew the raindrops in every direction, spraying her face and seeping into her clothing.

As she approached what had once been an intersection, she remembered to check the charge on her hover belt. The battery indicator was alarmingly red, and she had four waterways to cross before she got home. There wouldn't be enough charge.

This part of the city had been the hardest hit, shop owners going out of business to either move closer to the higher city center or away from the city entirely, into drier parts of the country. They'd only kept the ferry stop here because people still lived nearby. They just had to travel farther and farther to reach their jobs or their schools.

Kinuyo considered her options, standing on the sidewalk in a puddle that was at least five centimeters deep. She didn't know how long she'd have to wait here in the damp and cold before someone else came along who might be able to help her get home. It could be hours.

A bolt of lightning pierced the cloud cover, illuminating her reflection and something orange amid the gray.

In the center of the nearest intersection sat a rowboat, the lurid orange the rental shop owner in her neighborhood painted his boats so he could identify them if they were stolen or "misplaced." She didn't understand why anyone would rent a boat. People either owned a boat or took the ferries, cars and buses having been made obsolete by the flooding. She and her dad were ferry commuters, as he had deemed a boat a frivolous expense.

The sidewalks in this area were new, attached to what had once been the second floor of the buildings. The first floors were all submerged, along with the old infrastructure. One step off a sidewalk meant a plunge into six or more meters of frigid water. She wasn't a strong enough swimmer to brave the currents of the waterways.

But if she could bring this rowboat to her, her uncharged hover belt wouldn't matter.

She'd seen fishermen throw ropes toward stray boats to snag the ends, like the videos she'd seen of ranchers lassoing cattle, but she had neither rope nor rope handling skills.

She did have her yo-yo.

She maneuvered as close as she dared to the boat, the water lapping over her shoes. She knew better than to let it reach her knees, the point at which her stability would be threatened. She side-armed a throw, skipping the disc of her yo-yo across the water, aiming for a point beyond the boat, despite the insufficient length of her string.

The resultant splash radiated out until it reached the boat, which rocked in the wake.

Kinuyo grinned. She flung her yo-yo toward the boat again and again, each time pushing the boat a little farther. Her throws were fast and furious, the string staying dry through the sheer friction of the body riding the string with each throw and return.

Despite the precision of her throws, the boat remained near the center of the waterway. She needed to change its direction if she wanted it to reach the sidewalk.

One by one, she tried all the yo-yo tricks in her arsenal. As she did, she swore the string stretched longer with each attempt. It wasn't meant to stretch. She'd have to replace it when this was all done. (She dreaded her dad complaining about yet another frivolous expense.)

She threw the yo-yo again, releasing it with the necessary spin to turn it into a sleeper, if it were in the air. Instead, the yo-yo impacted the surface of the waterway and spun atop the water. The rotation acted like a propeller blade, giving the boat a burst of momentum. The string curved, against Kinuyo's will and the laws of physics, pushing the boat in the correct direction to reach the sidewalk.

Kinuyo tugged the string to bring the yo-yo back to her hand before she ran down the sidewalk to where the boat would arrive. The body of the yo-yo hummed with warmth despite having spun atop the water for at least a full minute. She wished someone else had been present to film the trick, so that she could prove she'd done such a thing.

But as she grasped the edge of the boat, she decided wrangling a boat to get her home from the ferry stop was a good enough reward for her amazing display of skills.

Yokai Hunters

Hitomi and Ayaka cornered me before the end of lunch.

"We've got the app working. Can you get your dad's car tonight?" Hitomi asked, slender arms crossed over her chest.

Beside her, Ayaka mimicked her pose, flicking quick glances at Hitomi and subtly adjusting.

I didn't dare look at either of them for very long. "Uh, yeah, sure," I mumbled, finally looking away. I pulled my phone out and looked at the screen. Comfortable spring temperatures, clear skies, full moon. "Wait, tonight? Are you sure?"

"What, afraid there will be werewolves after us?" Hitomi asked, her tone mocking.

Ayaka shook her head once, then pushed her glasses back up her nose from where they'd slid. "Statistical probability of werewolves existing and following the patterns ascribed to them in popular media is less than point-oh-six percent, Daichi."

I tried not to stare at her. "Point-oh-six is still within the realm of statistical possibility."

Hitomi rolled her eyes. "Nerds. You in or you out?"

I nodded, hoping it would hide me shaking in fear.

~

We called ourselves the Yokai Hunters on the internet, though we never spoke those words aloud off camera. We'd gone to great lengths to ensure no one would realize a popular girl like Hitomi spent her evening hours hunting for legendary spirits with two of the nerdiest people in our class. But Ayaka was a programming genius, and she and Hitomi knew I could borrow my dad's old Volvo whenever I wanted. Also, neither of them had their license, and I was good at driving them where they wanted to be when they wanted to be there.

We all wore baseball caps pulled low to cover our faces. Ayaka ditched her glasses and wore makeup, while Hitomi pulled her ponytail through the back of her baseball cap and donned a fake pair of glasses with a built-in camera.

We didn't set out to be famous on the internet, either. I recorded one of our first chases on my phone, using the app Ayaka had written to detect the spiritual energies of the yokai and project them onto our phone screens as animated sprites. To all the world, it looked like we were playing an augmented reality mobile game, until the app crashed, and I kept filming Hitomi capturing a malevolent manifested yokai. When we sat down to watch the replay, we agreed Ayaka could upload it to the internet, to see what happened.

Thirty-two hundred hits on the first video.

We now had eighteen thousand fans and climbing after every hunt.

That was enough to keep us going.

~

Tonight, Ayaka had located a yatsukahagi.

"A giant spider," Hitomi said, her voice flat. "Are you frickin' kidding me?"

Ayaka shrugged. "It needs to be stopped."

"I know," Hitomi grumbled. "Doesn't mean I have to like this job."

"What do we know about yatsu—giant spiders?" I asked. I was nothing if not woefully underinformed about the yokai. For my family, they were ancient mythology, left behind after my grandparents had left Japan. Except, as it turned out, the yokai were real.

"Like Hitomi said, giant spiders," Ayaka replied, her attention focused on the app. "Turn left at the next intersection."

"How do we stop them, I mean?" I asked, complying with her directions.

"Decapitation by katana, piercing with an iron spike, tossing it into running water." Hitomi rattled off the list, then shook her head. "Ugh, you guys have turned me into a nerd with an encyclopedic knowledge of monsters."

I sighed. "Did you happen bring a katana or an iron spike?"

"No, because you told me I couldn't keep an armory in your dad's trunk," Hitomi replied. "Swing by the hardware store. I'll find something."

~

Ayaka and I sat in the car while Hitomi shopped. I wanted to strike up a conversation, but the thought of doing so made my hands damp and clammy. Not the best way to begin a conversation, or to drive. I wiped my palms on my jeans.

Ayaka didn't seem to notice. She was busy applying makeup in the visor mirror.

Hitomi emerged from the hardware store with an improbably large bag, which she shoved behind my seat. She climbed into the car behind Ayaka and watched as Ayaka worked on her makeup. "You're so good at that. Why don't you wear makeup every day?"

Ayaka's expertly lightened eyebrows rose. "Why would I? This is a disguise. A costume. It's not who I am."

"But it looks good on you."

"If I started wearing makeup to school, we'd increase the odds of someone identifying me in the video. And the moment anyone identifies one of us, we're seventy-three minutes from them identifying you."

"How many minutes from identifying me?" I asked, my voice barely above a whisper.

"Roughly two hundred," Ayaka replied. "Your facial characteristics are much more common."

I breathed out a sigh of relief. "Thanks, I guess?" Then I took a deep breath before I continued. "Anyway, I'm with you. Why bother with the makeup if you don't want to wear it, right?"

Hitomi groaned. "Can we get on with this? I've got better things to do than listen to you two flirting."

"We're not flirting," Ayaka and I said in unison.

"Uh-huh. How much farther to the yatsukahagi?"

"Uh, turn right," Ayaka said.

I couldn't tell if she was looking at me or her phone, but I swung the car into the gravel alley behind a strip mall. My attention was now unwavering from the terrain ahead of us. Yokai didn't normally look like whatever creature they truly were—they disguised themselves somehow to blend in. But there were always tell-tale signs that something wasn't quite right about whatever form they took. I didn't have Hitomi's preternatural senses or Ayaka's app, but I was getting better at recognizing the yokai on sight.

Usually around the same time the girls started screaming for me to stop the car and start filming.

Ayaka hurled her phone at me before we'd even come to a complete stop, slinging her bulky backpack over one shoulder, and her door and Hitomi's were both open before I'd put the car in park.

Hitomi yanked something out of the hardware store bag. Meanwhile, I was having a hard time finding Ayaka's phone, which had bounced off my lap and fallen to the floorboards of the car, because I didn't want to take my eyes off the yatsukahagi.

At first, it looked sort of like a feral sheepdog, with overly long hair stained black and brown with filth and the outdoors. But if I averted my gaze even the slightest bit, I could see it for what it really was—a spider the size of a large dog, dark fuzz sticking up in all directions from its body and legs, and a demonic face.

A machete arced through the headlight beams, blocking my view of the yatsukahagi for long enough to break my horrified trance. I spotted Ayaka's phone and picked it up, wedging it between the windshield and the dashboard to get the AR display in view, and then grabbed my phone to start filming.

"Uh, Yokai Hunters here, and we're on the trail of a—" I paused to sound out the word correctly. "A ya-tsu-ka-ha-gi—yatsukahagi—a giant spider."

Outside the car, both Hitomi and Ayaka were chasing the yatsukahagi, Hitomi with her brand-new machete and Ayaka with a piece of what looked like rebar, which she wielded like a spear. Her left hand was clenched around more pieces of rebar, and I breathed a sigh of relief. Maybe she'd be able to throw the rebar and keep her distance from the yokai.

Ayaka surged ahead of Hitomi, thrusting the rebar in her right hand against the yatsukahagi's carapace. With the doors to the car still wide open, I heard the yatsukahagi screech, but it skittered away from Ayaka, seemingly unhurt.

Hitomi rushed past Ayaka and hacked at what looked the yatsukahagi's front legs, and the yatsukahagi darted out of sight.

The girls were at the far range of my headlights, and I knew our footage was going to be unusable if I didn't get moving. I tried to keep my phone steady as I reached over to close the front passenger side door.

There was no way I could close the back door. I'd have to hope the old hinges would be wobbly enough that the door would shut when I accelerated. Or I had to hope I wouldn't have to go down any narrow alleys. My dad would keep letting me borrow his car as long as I brought it back unscathed. If it got banged up or scratched up, all bets were off.

The girls were gone when I looked back in their direction, though Ayaka's backpack lay in the space between my headlights, less bulky than it had been when she'd leapt out of the car.

The way I saw it, I had two choices. I could drive toward where I'd seen them last and hope they'd just ducked out of the headlight beams. Or I could panic and leave the car, assuming the worst had happened.

At least I turned off the car before I ran.

I reached the end of the alley, where one of the buildings ended, forming a weird sort of courtyard between it and some other nearby buildings. Most of the overhead lights were burned out, but one cast a sickly pale yellow across the area.

Just enough for me to see Ayaka lying on the ground, limp, and Hitomi nowhere in sight.

"Ayaka!" I screamed, running toward her.

She twitched slightly, opening her eyes and shaking her head. But I'd already reached her side. "Daichi, I'm supposed to be bait."

"Bait?" I was going to kill Hitomi.

"Duck," Ayaka said, pulling me down beside her.

I felt the yatsukahagi's hair brush across my back, sending shivers across my entire body. My hand found one of the pieces of rebar Ayaka had been carrying, and I launched myself toward the yokai.

I had no idea what I thought I was going to do. I wasn't the fighting part of this team. Neither was Ayaka. But she'd charged toward the yokai every time, no matter what. I could do at least that much and hope Hitomi was about to sweep in to Ayaka's rescue. Or my rescue, now.

The yatsukahagi shied away from the rebar and scuttled sideways, as though it was trying to get around behind me.

I checked the opposite direction to make sure it wasn't working as a team with something else. Finding nothing there, I rotated with the yatsukahagi, keeping my gaze trained on it.

If it kept moving in the direction it was going, it might get back to where Ayaka was. Hopefully she'd moved by now, but I wasn't about to risk it.

I lunged toward the yatsukahagi, stabbing it with one end of the rebar. Once it started shrieking again, it was easier to ignore the squelching sound it made when I pierced its hide.

I really don't know what came over me, but I lifted the yatsukahagi with the rebar.

"Don't lose it!" Ayaka shouted.

I had been thinking about flinging it off into the dimly lit brushland behind the buildings, but I paused. "What do you want me to do with it, then?"

"Running water. There's a spigot on the next building down. That's where Hitomi went with the first one."

"First one? There's multiple?"

"Three, we think," Ayaka said. "Quick, running water."

I ran toward the building, still carrying the yatsukahagi on my piece of rebar. I was sure I looked ridiculous.

But it didn't matter. I'd left my phone and Ayaka's in the car. No one was filming.

Hitomi was going to be pissed.

The spigot was already on, a steady stream of water flowing from it. I thrust the yatsukahagi beneath it like I was sticking a marshmallow into a campfire. The effect was about as satisfying, as the yatsukahagi shriveled up as soon as the water hit it. It didn't even take a minute before my rebar was glistening clean.

Hitomi sauntered up and tossed two pieces of yatsukahagi, cleanly split with her machete, under the spigot. "What are you doing out here?" Her gaze landed on the rebar. "You got one?"

"Yeah, the one you left to get Ayaka," I said, feeling suddenly brave.

"I was going to come back and deal with it." She jerked her head back in the direction she had come from. "One of its buddies was hiding out over there, though."

Footsteps behind me made me whirl around, rebar still at the ready.

Ayaka's face was lit by a tablet screen, her lips pressed into a tight line. "Looks like we're clear over here."

"Wait a sec," Hitomi said. "If Daichi was fighting, who was filming?"

"No one," I said. "Sorry. When I lost track of you, I panicked."

"Not true," Ayaka said, swiping her fingers across her tablet. "I set up some backup so we could get more shots."

Something that looked like a miniature sci-fi spaceship whirred down near Ayaka.

"You got a drone?" I asked.

"I built a drone, thank you very much. No audio, but that's okay, since I don't think Hitomi wanted you yelling her name on camera."

I blushed, glad for the dim lighting. "Yeah, I'm not really cut out for this whole secret mission monster killing stuff."

Hitomi laughed. "Yeah, probably not. But you're our wheelman. Slash backup cameraman, slash backup monster killer." She paused and smiled. "If you're not too chicken."

I looked at the still running spigot, washing away whatever was left of the yatsukahagi away, out of our lives. Even so, it wouldn't be the last yokai we'd have to deal with. And whether I actually wanted to fight them or not, I knew I couldn't just walk away from Ayaka and Hitomi. They were on a mission, and I was too.

"Nope, you're stuck with me," I said, grinning at them both.

Maija Spencer, Internet Witch

By now, I'm sure you've seen the advertisements for "Maija Spencer, Internet Witch," all over your social media. They've got lines that sound like they're pulled out of books that were popular in the eighties. Win friends! Influence people! Be your own parachute! (How does that even work?) With *magic*!

I'm here to tell you that Maija Spencer is a fraud.

First off, Maija isn't her real name. Her parents named her the far less exciting Maria. Don't believe me? I can produce a copy of her birth certificate. I know, I know, that's small potatoes. People change their name all the time for stuff. It's just one of Maija's many lies.

Second off, there's no such thing as internet witches. This isn't like those internet churches, where you can get ordained on the internet to perform weddings and stuff.

Third off, the so-called "spells" she's offering to enact for people aren't even spells. She says you can be lucky in love, or get a good grade on your test, or whatever, and sure, she's got plenty of testimonials that say her magic works, but it's not magic.

It's social engineering.

Have you noticed that all her testimonials come from students (and faculty, though Hecate knows how she's pulled that off) at Lincoln High School? If you go to a different high school, have you tried to procure her services and been told she's "not taking any new clients"? That's because she's got no social capital anywhere but Lincoln High School.

And I'm here to knock that social capital out.

Maija Spencer, internet witch, is none other than Maria Hake. Who, you may ask? Exactly. Maria Hake is a nobody. But she's amazing at manipulating people around her. A few softly spoken words here, a few cleverly forged notes there, and all of a sudden, that boy you've always had a crush on is looking your way, not sure why, but he's intrigued. The math teacher grading the test you've been dreading? Suddenly grading leniently. It's math! There are rules! Not leniency!

You may be asking yourself, as you're reading this exposé, who is this anonymous author? Why do they have such a grudge against Maija?

And I'll tell you why. Because Maija Spencer gives real witches a bad name. She makes everyone think that witchcraft is just something easy you can accomplish by sending a small donation her way.

That's not how it works.

It's years of study, sweat, and yes, even a little blood. And the effects are minor, if you're lucky. If you wind up with a major effect, you'd better be prepared to duck and cover, because things are not going to go your way for much longer. Whatever you enact comes back to you, three times bigger, and three times worse.

This exposé is Maija Spencer's "three times bigger, and three times worse." Don't waste your money on her. She can't get you the results that real magic can.

You wouldn't want those results anyway.

Originally published in *Page & Spine*, November 2020.

He Who is in the Place of Embalming

It's a trick of the light
that the young mortician's
dim shadow resembles
the Jackal-headed god.
Or so I tell myself
to keep my fears at bay.

That doesn't explain why
he keeps a set of scales
tucked in the corner
of his gold-draped office,
nor why his onyx eyes
show me a darkened path.

Come with me, says his gaze,
a come-hither look.
He shows me quietude,
tranquility, repose,
an end to mortal cares.
Unending serenity.

I fear he's read me wrong.
I am not the dead girl
in this story. I am bereaved.
I am abandoned.
But I have no desire
to follow you to death.

Originally published in *The Weird and Whatnot*, August 2020.

Despite All My Rage

I wasn't kicked out of my house because I had the Gift. I was kicked out because I couldn't use it right.

My mom is on the Mage Council, so she trained me herself for years. Until the Testing.

Yeah, it's always the Testing.

I flunked. I could ace the concrete knowledge parts. I'd had those drilled into my brain. I just wanted to make my Gift my own, and for that, they flunked me.

My mother was livid. "How could you have failed? You have had the best of tutors!"

I shrugged. Any answer I could give her wouldn't be what she wanted to hear.

"Your failure reflects on *me*. It reflects on the entire Mage Council. This cannot stand."

She waved her hand, and I felt myself shrinking, shifting, changing. Mother's vanity meant there were mirrors everywhere, so I saw what she'd done. I was a rat.

"Leave." She pointed at the door. "You are my child no more. You are welcome here no more."

At least she turned me into a rat person. Still got opposable thumbs, which means I can still use my Gift. She couldn't take that away, no matter how much she might have wanted to.

I found other kids like me, tossed aside because they weren't "right." Not turned into rats. And that's made socializing awkward, because other kids don't really expect a four-foot bipedal rat to chat them up.

There are some who see past the awkward, see past me being a rat, and see in me the same rage that burns in them.

The ones the Mage Council has deemed unfit. The ones who have "not lived up to their potential." The ones who failed their arbitrary Testing.

So what do we do?

We rig the results. We corrupt the scores. We ensure the Testing doesn't run as planned. We burn the system down from the inside, as the unnoticeable, as the janitors and secretaries and cogs in the machine.

When the cogs stop, the machine stops.

Except for when it doesn't.

They still administer the Testing.

We don't think the results were ever real. They certainly aren't now.

So we'll try another way.

You think we can't do it? You think they'll stop us? They don't know how or when or where we'll hit them. They don't think like we do.

This is their weakness. They think that they're in control. They think that dictating the way the Gift works will keep the sheep in line.

They're wrong.

They've failed to see the signs around them. They've failed to keep up with the times. There are more of us every day.

Right under their noses, and right under yours, we've infiltrated the words, the music, the visuals. The things that you don't pay a lick of attention to every day.

Except for now, as we pound it into your subconscious.

And so you hear this song, you hear the drums and the guitars and the bass and the guttural screams. You hear it for what it is.

This is not a protest song.

This is your last warning.

We are coming.

This is war.

Originally published in *A Punk Rock Future*, October 2019.

The Adversary (Two Stilted Crowns)

———————

Who hath
wrought this awful
change? It is the man they
call the Adversary, for none
know his

true name,
nor where he comes
from. But he hath caused this
Silent Time, and we know not his
true aim.

In his
tower aloft
he bides his time. Alone
he knows, he sees, he hears the world.
He speaks,

whispers,
his will to those
who, silent, listen for
his commands. Find the girl who can
stop us.

She is
the only one who can upon
us bring ruin, failure,
calamity,
and death.

Even
he knows not how
she will accomplish such
a feat, but she alone holds his
downfall.

She who
knows so little
of who she is, and who
it is that she is destined to
become.

She has
her guides, while he
holds none close to him, for
he cannot trust a living soul
with his

knowledge.
Too costly bought,
a trade that proved worthy,
for Chaos turned overnight to
Order,

matters
not, for in the end of things, he
will burn, suffer, and weep
lament all, while
she flies.

One, Two, Three, FOUR!

Alan Brightman wasn't dead, but by the looks on the faces of the other boys at Tesiton Academy of the Arcane, you'd have thought he was. The third-year boy was curled in the fetal position at the foot of the grand staircase, gently weeping, awaiting his parents' arrival. The whispers on the stairs said he'd flunked out or been expelled. And while no one could agree on which of those it was, they knew the reason behind it. Alan Brightman had lost his magic.

Nigel stood beside Graham, who had started at Tesiton a year behind him, but who'd become Nigel's best friend in short order. They didn't join in the rumor mongering, but they also couldn't tear their eyes away from the wreck of a boy below.

"What do you suppose happened?" Graham asked, his voice soft.

Nigel shrugged. "I dunno, mate. No one's ever told me you could lose magic before today." He paused, considering. "Maybe no one ever has before. Least of all here."

"I don't think the teachers know either," Graham said. "They're standing over there like he's contagious, like it's something they can catch."

With a shudder, Nigel said, "We don't know that it's not, do we, now?"

Graham shuddered in response but recovered a moment later. "Do you think they'll change the room assignments? Maybe then we can bunk together?"

Nigel shook his head and ruffled Graham's mop-top hair. "You're still a first year, Graham. It's the barracks for you until you're second year. Anyway, he's a third year. Won't mean anything to the rest of us, unless they make new rules as a result."

As though Nigel's words had summoned him, Headmaster Clarkewood stepped between the stairs and Alan Brightman, blocking the other students' view of the boy with his not inconsiderable stoutness. "Gentlemen, that's enough lollygagging. Return to your rooms and attend to your studies. We will assemble in the chapel tomorrow morning and proceed with coursework from there."

A chorus of groans resounded on the stairs, but the boys did as they'd been told, ascending toward their rooms.

Nigel paused on the landing when they reached Graham's floor. "Be careful, mate. Can't have you losing your magic, eh?"

Graham nodded solemnly. "You too."

~

At breakfast the next morning, rumors about the nature of Alan Brightman's magic loss were flying.

"He kissed a toad and it took his magic!"

(The younger boys were disgusted by the idea of kissing anything or anyone, much less a toad. The older boys were certain *they* wouldn't kiss a toad, but they joked that some of their mates might not ever get a kiss if they didn't try out some toads.)

"He failed an exam and the teachers took his magic away as punishment."

(No wonder some of the boys were studying while they ate their porridge this morning. At least one boy sitting at the same table as Nigel and Graham was consulting the student handbook on the topic.)

"There's a walrus in the pond."

(Pond was a bit of an understatement, with the Tesiton Academy of the Arcane being located in a marshy region. During the rainy season, it was perhaps more accurately called a bog, or even a lake. All manner of strange creatures had been witnessed therein, and a further measure of even more unusual beings had been attested by the students as having been witnessed therein.)

But Nigel didn't understand why that had anything to do with Alan Brightman. So he turned to face Kent, the boy who had mentioned the walrus. "What?"

Kent wore owlish glasses, and the lights in the dining hall played across the smeared surface of said glasses in such a way that they obscured his eyes. "Walrus. In the pond. Stole Alan's magic."

Nigel looked around at the other boys at the table. Most of them were still chattering about the toad theory or the failure theory, expounding upon the relative merits of both. They'd either not heard Kent or shrugged off his suggestion. "How do you figure?"

Kent shrugged. "Alan liked to walk by the pond and skip stones on it. My guess is that he hit the walrus and it took his magic."

Graham piped up before Nigel could respond. "Do you mean an actual walrus, or something like a walrus?"

"Not sure," Kent replied. "Maybe something like. It sort of looks like a rock out there, but if you watch it for long enough, it moves."

Nigel pursed his lips, ready to disagree with Kent on the presence of a walrus, rock-like or otherwise, in a pond that was little more than a bog.

"I remember reading something about a creature like that," Graham said, his eyes shining.

"Really?" Nigel and Kent asked in unison.

Graham nodded. "I saw it when I was trying to choose a creature to write an essay about."

"What's it called, then?" Nigel asked.

"Don't remember."

"Tell you what." Kent jerked his chin toward Nigel. "I'll take you to see the walrus. Your friend here can go look up what it's called. And maybe how to stop it?"

"Aren't you worried about losing your magic, too?" Graham asked, suddenly pale. His gaze wavered between Kent and Nigel.

Nigel glanced at Kent, but the other boy's eyes betrayed nothing. "We'll be fine, Graham. See what you can find out about this thing in the pond."

~

The porch nearest the pond had an overhang, but such things barely mattered when the mistlike rain fell mostly sideways, rather than downward.

Nigel looked toward the pond. "Maybe we should just watch from here, not go tromping around in the rain and muck."

"We won't see anything from here," Kent said. "Gotta get closer."

Nigel bit at the inside of his lip but nodded. He wasn't sure this was any more plausible than toads or flunking, but between Kent's steely composure and Graham's enthusiasm about some sort of strange creature that could steal magic and might look like a walrus, here he was.

Kent and Nigel trudged through the mist and muck toward the pond. If they were truly fortunate, Nigel considered, no one would notice they hadn't been at chapel, there'd be nothing to see in the pond, and they'd get no mud on their shoes. He didn't relish the idea of being tasked with scrubbing the floors till they gleamed, the usual punishment for any manner of infractions at Tesiton.

"There it is," Kent said, pointing a shaking finger toward a rock near the center of the pond.

"That's a rock, mate. Been like that since I got here."

"You have to wait for it to forget we're here."

"How long do you suppose that'll take?"

Kent shrugged. "If it hasn't moved before they ring the first bell, we'll go inside."

Nigel pulled his arms inside the sleeves of his woolen sweater, rubbing them as he tried to stay warm. He felt the damp seeping into his shoes and socks, and he began to regret every decision in his life that had brought him to this point.

The rock shifted.

Nigel blinked, unsure he'd actually seen movement in the pond.

But Kent took a stumbling step backward.

The rock rose several inches. Faint light glimmered on the portion of it that had previously been below the surface of the pond.

Kent ran toward the school.

Nigel followed.

~

Graham had an answer for them by lunchtime. "Tusked Merula."

64

Nigel and Kent looked at one another. Nigel knew he hadn't seen the creature's face to verify tusks, and he suspected Kent hadn't either. But they had to tell Graham something. "What's it look like, then?" Nigel asked.

"Big, walrus-like thing, with a belly as black as coal when it's hungry for magic."

"Must not have been hungry," Kent murmured.

"Okay, good," Nigel said. "How do we stop it?"

"Well, it's got these big ear holes—" Graham held his hands together, making a circle with his thumbs and pointer fingers. "—that it can cover when it's underwater, but that opens when it surfaces."

"And how do we make it surface?" Kent asked.

"Vibrations," Graham replied. "And then we have to deafen it to stop it from stealing magic."

"Won't it starve if it can't eat magic?" Nigel asked. He didn't know why this was suddenly a concern, when this Tusked Merula had sent a boy home without magic, but he felt a twinge of pity when he thought about being prevented from eating a favorite meal.

"Naw, it can eat other things to live," Graham said. "It just likes to eat magic so it can do magic of its own. But it's basically a parasite."

That made the decision a little easier. "So how do you plan on us deafening this thing?"

Graham glanced around, then leaned close to the table before he whispered his answer, forcing Nigel and Kent to lean in too. "Do either of you have an amplifier?"

Amplifiers (and the guitars that went with them) were strictly not allowed at Tesiton Academy of the Arcane. But as Nigel shared a sidelong look with Kent, he began to wonder if the three of them were all inclined toward the same sort of troublemaking in the form of rock-n-roll.

"You?" Kent asked, jerking his chin toward Graham.

"Yeah, but keep it quiet like, right?"

Kent nodded. "Of course. So what's the plan?"

"We've got to find a way to get power out to the pond."

~

The boys had to wait for cover of darkness to run cables and amplifiers out of the school doors and across the marshy ground. They'd brought their rain slickers with them to place beneath the amps themselves, Kent and Nigel's matching Gibsons, and Graham's mustard yellow Fender. But Kent and Graham had the matched Gibson J-160E guitars, and they were busily comparing the different sounds that their respective amps provided, rather than watching the pond. Nigel stood watch, his right hand's fingers working over the frets on his Fender Esquire, practicing chords.

The surface of the pond was jet black under the cloudy night sky, but ripples flowed rhythmically across its surface. Nigel tuned the other two boys out and began to strum in time with the ripples, muffling the sound with the palm of his left hand.

The ground thrummed with the electrical vibrations, and as Nigel played, the ripples moved faster, the pond sloshing over its banks nearest to him.

He didn't realize what was happening until a dark figure parted the surface of the pond.

"That's it, that's it!" Graham half-whispered and half-shouted.

Nigel shook his head out of his reverie and gaped at the thing coming out of the lake. Had he not known better, he would have believed it really was a walrus, with long tusks glimmering in the faint power indicator lights of the amplifiers.

Two holes opened, one on either side of the Tusked Merula's head, just as big as Graham had indicated.

"Play!" Kent shouted.

"Play what?" Graham asked, panic evident in his voice.

"C," Nigel replied, his fingers already in position. "One, two, three, FOUR!"

It took the boys a moment until they found their rhythm, but then the chord rang out perfectly, and the Tusked Merula squealed.

But rather than diving back underwater, it began pulling itself out of the pond.

"Not working!" Kent shouted.

Nigel's fingers scrambled over the frets of his guitar. "Change it up. Add an E minor." He demonstrated what he was thinking, and a moment later, Kent and Graham joined in.

Somehow, the combination of the two chords blended into a sound that changed the Tusked Merula's howl, driving the creature off the shoreline and back into the pond.

The boys continued to play, even after the ripples in the pond diminished into virtual stillness.

Nigel looked toward Graham. "Well, did we do it?"

"I think so?" Graham looked unsure until his gaze flickered toward the school and he blanched. "I hope so."

Kent and Nigel turned their attention in the same direction, spotting the headmaster marching toward them. Several students filled the space between the doors to the yard, while others lurked at windows facing the pond.

"What in the name of Heaven is going on out here?" the Headmaster thundered.

All of Nigel's courage rose up in his throat and forced the words out. "Dealing with the Tusked Merula in the pond, Headmaster."

The Headmaster's gaze narrowed, one eyebrow arching in surprise, but he stopped stalking toward the boys. "Tidy up this mess you've created, and then I will speak with the three of you in my office about these contraband instruments and electrical devices."

~

Kent, Nigel, and Graham stood outside the Headmaster's office, having returned their guitars and amplifiers in their respective rooms. Even had they wanted to hide them away, they suspected every other boy in their class would ferret out the hiding places within an hour. And the odds were good that the Headmaster would march them back up to their rooms to confiscate their musical equipment anyway.

"Say, if the Headmaster doesn't take our guitars, what do you two fellas say to putting together a band?" Kent asked.

"What, just the three of us?" Graham asked. "Just three guitars?"

"I suspect we can find a drummer, now that half the school's seen what we can do."

"Who's going to sing?" Nigel asked.

Kent shrugged. "S'pose we'll have to try that out next, eh?"

"If the Headmaster doesn't take our instruments," Nigel reminded him.

"Leave that part to me," Kent said, a gleam in his eye.

Fire Bad

The candles burned bright amongst the shadows, and the young black cat, whose first family had called him Trouble, and whose second family named him Bubblefluff, was entranced.

"Aww, look! Bubblefluff likes the candles." The youngest daughter, Cindy, was the one who had named him, and she thought everything he did was adorable, sometimes in four separate words. A Dor A Ble.

"Keep an eye on him, Cin," her father said. "You don't want him to singe his whiskers." More quietly, but loud enough for Bubblefluff to hear, he muttered, "Or burn the house down."

Bubblefluff heard the words "singe" and "burn," and they conjured up such images in his head. A world consumed in flames like the one atop the candle. He didn't understand where the images had come from, but they drew him closer to the flame.

Cindy grabbed him and pulled him away. "No, Bubblefluff. Candles are bad."

Bubblefluff had heard "bad" many times. It was always the most interesting things that were bad. He remembered "bad" from his first family, too. Everything he did there was "bad." And then there had been a car ride to the cold place, and shivering, and then finally Cindy and her family, and a new name. And less "bad."

But he couldn't help his fascination with the candles. And Cindy was not, despite her father's admonition, keeping an eye on him. He moved closer to the flame.

In the sputtering of the wick, his keen hearing found out more words, interesting ones like "singe" and "burn." A song of the history of cats, from the time when they were larger, not domesticated. (Bubblefluff wasn't sure about that last word, but he thought he had heard it at the place of pokes and cheese that his humans called "the vet.") From a time when the other animals feared the cats and their mighty, fiery, roars.

Bubblefluff blinked slowly at the candle flame. Ever since the family had closed his favorite window, the house had been too warm. Now they had candles burning in a decorative device they had gotten down from the attic (entering the attic was also "bad"). And between the warmth and the hypnosis of the candle, he was getting sleepy.

It was about time for a nap, anyway. Cindy was reading a book on the couch. He bounded up beside her and climbed into her lap, turning around a few times before he found the most comfortable place to lay, nudging her book with his whiskers until she held it in the right position.

Bubblefluff watched the candle from a distance, for just a while longer. Then he blinked, once, twice, and then closed his eyes to dream of the days when cats breathed fire.

———

Originally published in *Page & Spine*, March 2020.

Motes and Morsels

―――――――――

They call her the Beldame of Brocker Lane,
but she's not a witch, nor ugly,
she's just not like the rest of them,
and they can't abide differences.

She spends her days peering through a microscope,
studying the animacules that no one notices,
cataloguing morsels of every little thing,
naming each one like children.

When she realizes the delivery driver
is the same every week,
she tries to make small talk,
his blush more incarnadine than her own.

She wants to know more about him,
but she's not good at asking questions of people.
She studies the motes he leaves behind
and finds the essence of him.

It's a funny little courtship,
and she wonders what they'll call him,
when he ends all his delivery runs
at their home on Brocker Lane.

―――――――――

Originally published in *Apparition Lit*, January 2020.

Full Weekend Pass

Moonflower stumbled as she stepped out of the portal. Her hair fell in front of her face like a veil. Beneath her hands, the floor was rough and fibrous. One deep breath assured her that the spell had worked. The air was foul with artificial odors. Moonflower smiled, even as the smell crinkled her nose.

She rose and tucked her hair behind her ears. The room around her was dark. "Golau," she intoned, but the anticipated light did not appear. She tried again, focusing her full will into the word. The darkness persisted despite her efforts.

Moonflower turned back to the portal, which hung open, visible in spite of the darkness. She frowned and gestured at it. "Cau." Nothing changed. "Bloody hell."

She forced her feelings of panic back down, resolved to complete what she had come here to do. A thin sliver of light at ground level showed her where the door was. She moved toward it and fumbled for a doorknob.

The light in the hallway blinded Moonflower for an instant, and she blinked to adjust. The convention-goers in the hallway were raucous and barely noticed her entry. She glanced at the number on the door she had come out of, before she realized that it had locked behind her. That would make getting back home more difficult than she had anticipated.

Moonflower crept through the hallways of the hotel, trying not to draw attention to herself. But at nearly every step, another person nodded or smiled at her, or told her they liked her "costume." One girl even complimented her on how real her ears looked.

She looked back over her shoulder as she walked. She had not spotted any of the palace guards, but it would not be long before her father noticed that she was missing. His elite warriors were sure to find her and bring her home.

Moonflower's forward motion stopped abruptly at a spongy wall. When she looked up, she found herself looking at one of the other convention-goers. He was more than six feet tall, wearing synthetic furs and plastic armor, and carrying an axe that looked like it was carved from Styrofoam. Moonflower wrinkled her nose. "Are you supposed to be a dwarf?"

The man scowled at her. "Yes."

"You're a little tall for a dwarf," she muttered. As she hurried away, she fumbled for the hood of the cloak that she wasn't wearing. Being invisible would have made this easier.

Moonflower turned the corner, looking for a place where she could hide for a few hours. She ducked through the first open doorway she saw.

"Oh look, Stacey, another Moonflower." A woman's voice cut through the buzz of conversation, her tone dripping with sarcasm. "I don't know why they don't just give up and call this MoonflowerCon."

Moonflower turned to look for the woman. A handful of costumed convention-goers sat in chairs facing the front of the room, where TV screens advertised "The Language of Deyrnas." A pair of women stood, facing her, with their arms crossed over their chests. Both were dressed exactly like her, down to the stick straight blonde hair (natural on one, an obvious wig on the other), elven ears, and white bell-sleeved gown.

"You know me, then?" Moonflower asked.

The woman wearing the blonde wig scoffed. "Know you? No. We recognize your costume, that's all."

Moonflower shook her head. "No, don't you see? I *am* Moonflower."

The women both laughed. "Sure you are," said the woman in the wig. Turning her attention away from Moonflower, she spoke to the other woman. "I've got to get to my next panel. I'll see you later."

Moonflower watched the first woman walk off. The other woman, the one called Stacey, lingered. "It's a great costume. You do look a lot like her," she said.

Moonflower sighed. "That's because I am her. I was invited to meet someone, and here was the best place for us to meet. I couldn't exactly bring him into Deyrnas."

"Right," Stacey agreed. "Of course not. Umm ... how exactly did you get here?"

"I found a spell in one of the Forbidden Tomes that opens a portal to another world."

Stacey furrowed her brow. "You are aware that 'Deyrnas' is just a game, right?"

"I understand that in this realm, it is a game. But I'm living proof that it is also a real place. And I'm here to prove to Lord Kiernan Blacksword that it's real."

Stacey paled. "Kiernan Blacksword? You ... you know him?"

"I haven't met him in person yet. That's why I'm here."

Stacey fidgeted with her hair. "Okay, is there anything you can do to prove you are who you say you are?"

"I have the Mwclis," Moonflower said, touching the choker she wore.

"Oh, is that how you pronounce that?" Stacey laughed. "Okay, not bad. But they make replicas of that." She indicated her own choker.

"I suppose they make replicas of most everything I wear," Moonflower said, looking over Stacey's costume. "And my magic doesn't seem to work here."

"Your magic works in Deyrnas? Oh, right, of course it does. Your portal."

"Yes. I couldn't close it, but I don't think we can get back into the room where it is. And I couldn't make light in the room. Watch." Moonflower placed her left hand out, palm up. "Tān," she whispered.

Stacey stared at Moonflower's hand. Moonflower hazarded a glance downward and saw only the faintest lick of flame at the center of her hand, giving off no heat. "The magic must be leaking through the portal!"

"Okay, I'll help you find Kiernan," Stacey said. "Just ... put that out before someone notices, okay?"

~

"Hey, twin Moonflowers! Will you pose together?"

Moonflower glared at the man who had made the request. Stacey leaned toward her and whispered. "Just go with it."

"What? Why?" Moonflower asked. Stacey slung her arm around Moonflower's shoulders and posed.

The man took a picture and checked the view screen on his camera. "Um, thanks," he muttered, eyes still fixed on the screen.

"Stacey, I don't want to draw attention to myself. Stopping for pictures is not a good way to be stealthy."

"I know, but refusing to stop for pictures is a good way to draw attention to ourselves." Stacey shrugged. "Costumed people get asked for pictures all the time. It's just how it works. Your only option to avoid it is to change clothes."

Moonflower frowned. "I didn't bring any other clothes."

"I've got something that will fit you, I think. C'mon, let's go."

The girls turned the corner and Moonflower gasped. She grabbed Stacey's arm and yanked her back. "Ow! What?" Stacey exclaimed.

"I just saw one of the palace guards," Moonflower whispered.

Stacey poked her head around the corner. "It's just another costume."

"How can you be sure?"

"I can't," Stacey said with a shrug. "But then again, I can't really be sure that you're Moonflower."

Moonflower hesitated. "What is your name in Deyrnas?"

Stacey blushed. "Oh, um, Phoenix Ravenborn."

"You're a priestess of Iachau, though you've been noted by your order as a frequent visitor to the temple of Hydref recently," Moonflower began.

Stacey interrupted her. "Okay. Convinced. You're either Moonflower or a sysadmin."

Moonflower smiled. "I'm Moonflower. The palace guards are the sysadmins."

"So they're human?"

"Ah, yes, some of them. But they have analogues within the game, too, that are real within the game world. It gets a bit complicated."

"Right," Stacey said. "I get the impression that all of this is complicated. So that guard down the hall, did he follow you out of the portal or was he already here?"

"I can't be sure. Either way, I'd rather avoid a confrontation with him. I want to find Kiernan."

"Yeah, about that." Stacey hesitated and frowned.

Moonflower studied Stacey's face, but the other girl remained quiet. "You know him?"

"You could say that. I ran into him at a party last night. He thought I was you, that you had arrived early. He was kinda drunk. He kept professing his undying love to me. It was a little embarrassing."

Moonflower sighed. "Oh, how sweet!"

"Um, yeah." Stacey bit her lip. "He then proceeded to proclaim his undying love for every other woman in the room. He left with one of them."

"Oh," Moonflower said, the wind knocked out of her sails. "Oh. He had ... oh." Tears flowed down her cheeks.

Stacey reached over and hugged Moonflower. As she did, she spotted the palace guard looking in their direction. "I guess we should hide," Stacey whispered.

She tried the door they were standing in front of, and it opened. The girls ducked into the room. Five heads swiveled in their direction and stared. The inhabitants of the room were all male, and they were crowded around a small table. Strewn across the surface of the table were paper, pencils, and dice.

No one spoke for a long moment. Finally, Moonflower broke the silence, wiping away her tears. "Hello," Moonflower said. "Do you mind horribly if we ... um ... watch whatever it is that you're doing?"

One of the men turned to another. "Steven, why did two girls just walk into our game?"

Moonflower looked at Stacey, who rolled her eyes. "Hey, genius. You do realize that girls have ears, right?"

The man blushed. The one who he had called Steven stood up and cleared his throat. "Ah, can we help you?"

"We're just looking for a place where we can sit down for a little while," Stacey said. "And maybe borrow your computer, if you've got 'Deyrnas' on it."

"Yeah, Stefan does," Steven gestured to one of the other men. "Oh, right, introductions. We're the League of Steves. I'm Steven with a V, that's Stefan, Esteban, PH-Stephen, and Stevie."

"Wow," Stacey said. "Who knew Steve was such a versatile name? So what are you guys playing?"

"We're playtesting a tabletop version of 'Deyrnas'," Steven said. "Stefan wrote it."

Moonflower looked at the map laid out in the center of the table. "Would you like me to add the secret groves?"

Stefan looked up from his laptop and blinked at her. "No one in game knows where all of the secret groves are. People say they move around."

"They don't. If you want to know where they are, I can tell you."

"Riiiiiight." He turned his laptop around. "You wanted to log in?"

"No, I do," Stacey said. "Um, her account is, you know, borked right now."

"Yeah," Moonflower said. She leaned over Stacey's shoulder and whispered. "What are you doing?"

"I'm sending Kiernan a message that you've arrived. I'm going to tell him that you'll meet him in the lobby in an hour."

"Is that a good idea?"

Stacey grinned. "Maybe, maybe not. I have a plan."

~

Moonflower scratched at her wrist. Stacey had provided her with a change of clothing, but the fabric felt strange on Moonflower's skin. At least wandering the convention in Stacey's clothes had drawn all attention away from Moonflower. It was the perfect disguise.

"He's here," Stacey whispered from her position in the lobby. Moonflower had given her an amulet that allowed them to communicate across the space. Moonflower looked up to see a young man approach Stacey. He was dressed exactly like Lord Kiernan Blacksword appeared in Deyrnas, though he was just barely taller than Stacey. In her home realm, Lord Blacksword was easily a foot taller than Moonflower.

Kiernan looked at Stacey. "How do I know that I'm speaking with the real Moonflower?"

"Because you pledged your sword to me on the feast of Gwanwyn past," Moonflower murmured. Stacey repeated Moonflower's words to Kiernan.

He looked around frantically to see if anyone had overheard Stacey's words. After a moment he took her hand. "Milady. I am honored that you have made the journey from Deyrnas to my home realm. Let us not speak of pledges past, but only of pledges present. I pledge my undying—"

"Do not speak of such things here, Lord Blacksword," Stacey said. "If you wish to make a new pledge to me, it cannot be in this realm. It must be in Deyrnas."

Kiernan frowned. "Why did you make the journey, if not to accept my pledge in person?"

"I came here to ... prove to you that I could," Stacey stammered.

"Tell him because his faith was weak," Moonflower suggested.

"And because your faith was weak."

Kiernan dropped to one knee before Stacey. "Now that you are here, I wish to persuade you to remain." He fumbled beneath his tunic and produced a small box.

"Oh crap," Stacey muttered, only loud enough for Moonflower to hear.

Conversations around the lobby stopped, and all attention focused on Stacey and Kiernan. Stacey's face had gone pale, with bright spots of color high on her cheeks. She looked like she wanted to run.

"Is that a ring?" Moonflower asked Stacey. The other girl simply nodded, her eyes wide and mouth agape. "It's probably enchanted with some sort of magic of this realm. Don't touch it. I'm coming out."

As Moonflower moved toward the humans, she spotted Haedirn, one of her father's elite guards. Before she could call out to Stacey, Haedirn and several other guards moved into position around Stacey and Kiernan.

"Real?" Stacey asked quietly.

Moonflower nodded, and then remembered that her gestures would not carry through the communication amulet. "Yes, real. Real trouble. His name is Haedirn."

Moonflower slipped back into the crowd. Several of the people had phones out and were taking pictures or video.

Haedirn touched Stacey on the shoulder, and she wheeled around. "Unhand me, Haedirn!"

"Your Highness," Haedirn said with a bow. "Your Lord Father has asked us to accompany you back to Deyrnas."

"But I don't want to return to Deyrnas right now. I'm ... I'm having a lovely time here with all of these people."

Haedirn's brow furrowed. "But your Lord Father—"

"Can take this matter up with me," Kiernan interrupted.

Haedrin looked down at Kiernan. The guard towered a full head taller than the young man. "King Brenin does not fear you, Lord Blacksword. You will fall beneath his blade in a matter of seconds."

Kiernan reached for his sword, but Stacey stayed his arm. "You don't want security to come down on our heads too, do you?" she hissed at Kiernan. "Play along with these guys. They're just cosplayers." Then she turned back to Haedrin. "We shall accompany you." She dropped her voice down to a whisper. "Moonflower, they can't really take us back, right?"

"If they can, then things have become very strange in this realm."

~

Moonflower weaved through another group of convention-goers, muttering apologies as she passed between them. She could just barely see the plumes of the palace guards' helmets above the crowd.

"Stacey," she murmured. "I'm having a hard time catching up to you. Find out how the guards plan on getting you back to Deyrnas."

Before Stacey had a chance to say anything, Moonflower caught a snippet of a conversation near her new friend. "—the couple with the proposal in the lobby? Can we get your picture?"

"Oh, yes, of course," Stacey replied. "Haedirn, you should be in the picture as well."

Haedirn stammered for a few moments, his words unintelligible over the communications amulet. But Moonflower could see the plumes stop, and she squeezed between a group of girls with dragon puppets on their shoulders to get closer to Stacey and Kiernan.

Just as quickly as she had gained ground, the guards moved again. Three of the guards moved into a wedge formation and began parting the crowd, while one guard followed behind them, at a distance. Though she couldn't see Stacey and Kiernan, she assumed they must be immediately in front of the guard in the back.

"Is that Haedirn behind you?" she asked.

A moment passed before Stacey responded. "Oh, yeah, you can't hear me if I nod."

Moonflower thought about the cameras she had seen various people carrying, and intoned, "Dyfais." She felt a small weight settle into her hand. The camera looked old and clunky, but she didn't need it to be functional.

"Haedirn," she called out, pitching her voice higher. She held the camera up in front of her face before he turned. "Can I get a picture? Your costume is great."

The guard frowned, but he stopped moving. Moonflower took a few steps forward, turning the camera to cover her mouth. "Stacey, grab Kiernan and run," she muttered just before she pressed the button atop the camera.

"Hey, stop!" one of the other guards shouted. Haedirn spun around and moved to intercept Stacey's panicked flight.

"Sorry, no more photos," Haedirn growled at Moonflower. He placed a hand on Stacey's shoulder and gestured at Kiernan with his spear.

Moonflower tried to will the camera away, but it stayed in her hand. She tucked it halfway into the waistband of her borrowed jeans to free her hands, and called out to Haedirn. "Hey, you've got the wrong girl!"

Haedirn turned back to her. "Nice try," he began, but recognition dawned on his face as soon as he saw Moonflower without the camera obscuring her face. He recoiled a step back. "Your Highness, what are you wearing?"

Moonflower shrugged. "That's not important. How are you planning on getting them back to Deyrnas? They're both human."

"Your Lord Father has provided us with a way. He anticipated the need to bring your companion back." He nearly spat the last few words out.

Moonflower scrutinized Haedirn for anything different about his appearance. Around his wrist, he wore a coiled golden bracelet, similar to one she had seen her father wear when he held court to try those accused of treachery.

"You don't need to bring him back," Moonflower said. She dropped her eyes and focused on the chaotic pattern of the carpet. "And you don't need to take her back, either. She was meeting with him for my protection. If you let them both go, I'll return with you."

Haedirn moved closer to Moonflower and took her hand. "Your Highness, your place is in Deyrnas." He turned back to the other guards and nodded. "Let the humans go."

As soon as Stacey and Kiernan had moved away from the guards, Moonflower looked up at Haedirn. "You're so gullible." She tapped the end of the coiled bracelet. "Ymlacio!"

The bracelet slithered down Haedirn's wrist, across their joined hands, and onto Moonflower's wrist. A brief pulse of power coursed through the supple metal as it settled onto her arm. She pulled free of Haedirn's grasp and waved her arm at him and the other guards. "You've got two choices. I can send you home now, with a message for my father that I'll be home in three days. Or you can stay here and enjoy the convention." She smiled. "They have an entire convention about our realm. It's rather flattering, really."

"If we return without you, it will be our heads," Haedirn said. "You know that, Your Highness."

"Perfect! Then stay here and have *fun*! You can tell my father that I was particularly elusive. I'll back you up on it."

Haedirn grimaced. "Fun?"

Moonflower sighed. "Yes. You should try it sometime, Haedirn."

"With all due respect, Your Highness, we must return."

"I will return at the end of the weekend," Moonflower said, her voice firm. "I will not stop you from going if that is your wish. But I certainly can't advise it."

Haedirn looked around, a frown creasing his brow. "Would you at least speak with your father, and assure him of your safety here?"

"Yes, I can do that. I suppose I'll need to log in to Deyrnas again." Moonflower looked at Stacey. "Could I use your account?"

Stacey nodded, wide-eyed. "Of course, Your Highness."

"No," Moonflower said, shaking her head. "You're my friend. I don't expect any deference from you, Stacey. Or should I call you Phoenix?"

"Either one is fine," Stacey replied with a grin. "Oh, but what about Kiernan?"

Moonflower stared at the young man. He stood apart from the guards, trying to blend in with the crowd. "How many girls?" she asked.

"Pardon?" he asked, his face pale.

"My friend Stacey tells me that you proclaimed your undying love to her last night. And then you proposed to her as well."

"But I ... I thought she was you!"

Moonflower scoffed. "Did you think that all of the girls at the party were me? Including the one you left with?"

Kiernan's face turned from pale to an astonishing shade of red. He stammered for a moment, then said, "I was drunk, milady."

Moonflower straightened her posture and looked down her nose at him. "The princess of Deyrnas does not make vows with one whose inebriation causes him to engage in ridiculous behavior. You are released from all previous vows. Or, in the words they use in this place, I'm dumping you."

Kiernan backed away slowly. Someone within the gathered crowd began clapping, and soon most of the women had joined in the applause, along with a good number of the men.

Stacey smiled at Moonflower as they walked away from Kiernan and the crowd, the guards trailing behind the two women.

"So what are you going to do after you've talked to your father?"

"I'm not sure." Moonflower hesitated. "Did you have any plans?"

"Not really. There's a dance tonight that I was thinking about going to."

"Then let's," Moonflower suggested. "Perhaps some of those Steves will be interested in dancing?"

"Maybe so," Stacey laughed. "And if not, I'm sure you can dance with any of the other guys here."

"I think I may be done with human men." Moonflower paused and watched another convention-goer pass by, this one dressed as an elven prince she could not identify. "Well, at least maybe after the weekend."

Memorandum from the Panel for the Identification of Consequentially Chosen Youth

It has come to the attention of the Panel for the Identification of Consequentially Chosen Youth, after recent failures of Chosen Ones to complete their appointed missions, that the once-stringent methodology employed by previous incarnations of this Panel have fallen by the wayside. We present to you an updated list of "don'ts" that should be considered when determining the best candidate to carry out any given prophecy to which you are privy.

1. Don't assume the Chosen One must be blonde haired and blue eyed. You're setting yourself up for inevitable failure. Only two percent of the world's population has blonde hair. Only eight percent have blue eyes. While the combination taken together is a common presentation of these phenotypes, the odds are astronomical that you can find someone meeting these criteria who is also the best person for the job. Put the job first, and the looks second.

2. Don't insist that all prophecies require cisgender young women to fill the role of Chosen One. Some of our recent success stories have employed transgender girls, non-binary folks, and gender non-confirming individuals as Chosen Ones. They just don't get as much press as the blonde cheerleaders who manage to save the day.

3. Which reminds me, don't select popular cheerleaders as Chosen Ones. While cheerleaders possess many admirable skills, "defeating evil" is not among them. They may be able to *encourage* the Chosen One to "fight," but they themselves are not the best candidates for taking the fight to the forces of evil. Besides which,

they often have grueling practice and game schedules, not to mention busy social calendars, which detract from the amount of time they can spend engaged in their mission.

4. Don't exclude the nerdy ones. In fact, we've seen better than an 80 percent success rate when selecting so-called "nerdy" Chosen Ones. What have they all had in common? They did their research before rushing headlong into danger. (The approximate 20 percent of nerdy Chosen Ones who failed to complete their missions faced extenuating circumstances. We can't expect them all to win. We can only hope that when they don't win, it's not the fate of the entire world resting on their shoulders.)

5. Don't expect your Chosen One to be ready to take on their mission immediately. Training is key to a successful mission completion. We understand that training montages are thematically appropriate and a real time-saver, but if you want your Chosen One to win the day, maybe take the time to, oh, I don't know, actually train them?

The Panel for the Identification of Consequentially Chosen Youth thanks you for your attention to this memorandum, and encourages you to reach out with any questions, comments, or concerns you may have on this topic.

———————

Originally published in *Page & Spine*, July 2020.

Safe Haven

2018
Lobby
8:38 PM

I'm used to guests rushing into the lobby at top speed, but the latest arrival put them all to shame. She less ran and more whirled in, as though she were a Tasmanian devil. Her long auburn hair was unkempt, and her clothes didn't seem to have fared much better on whatever journey had brought her to Hotel Stormcove. To top it off, she didn't even have luggage.

"I need a room," she gasped. Her gaze darted back and forth between the front desk and the glass of the entryway. "Interior. No windows."

I tapped a few keys on the computer at the check-in desk. "My apologies. We're in the midst of a software upgrade, Ms.—"

"Irwin. Sasha Irwin." She drummed her nails on the countertop, then stepped back from the desk, hiding her fingertips in clenched fists. "I'm in a bit of a hurry."

I pasted on my best smile. "Yes, of course. Just a few moments, I'm sure. Could I interest you in a cup of tea while you wait?" I asked.

She narrowed her eyes at me. "What's in it?"

"We have chamomile, mint, uhhh ... I think we may still have some others."

"Monkshood?" she asked.

I arched an eyebrow at her and shook my head. "No, I'm afraid not. It's not a popular tea flavor."

"Yeah, I suppose not." She paced, still glancing out the hotel doors occasionally. "D'ya have a smart phone?"

"Yes, ma'am."

That made her cringe. "Please don't call me ma'am. Miss Irwin is fine, but ma'am makes me think of my mum."

"Of course, Miss Irwin. Yes, I do have a smart phone."

"While your software's doing whatever it's doing, can you look up the time of moonrise tonight?"

I nodded. It was an odd request—not the oddest I've received working here, believe it or not—but also unnecessary. I tapped the employee schedule beside me. "I actually have that information handy. 8:43 p.m. this evening."

She looked at her wristwatch, then held it to her ear. "What time d'ya have?"

"8:40."

She grimaced. "How accurate is that?"

"It should be quite correct." The computer beeped, its software update complete. "Here we are. Interior room on the fifth floor alright with you?"

"Floor doesn't bother me."

"How many nights?"

"Five. No, make it six, just ... yeah, six."

I nodded. "Very good. And how will you be paying for your stay with us?"

Miss Irwin grimaced again and leaned over the counter. "Look, I don't want to be an imposition, but my understanding is this hotel provides accommodations to those in need?"

I made sure to lower my voice in response. "Yes, Miss Irwin, that is accurate."

"I'm in a dire need." She pulled a wad of bills from her pocket. "I've got a bit I've been squirreling away, but I don't think it's going to cover six nights."

"Management will, in fact, accept whatever payment you can make."

She smiled for the first time, revealing canines that put dogs to shame. "Thank you—" Her gaze passed across the nameplate on my chest. "—Alex."

I passed the keys to her across the desk. "Central elevator, no windows there either. You'll find your room just to the right of the elevator landing. If you find yourself in need of anything, just ring the front desk. I'll be heading off shift in a moment, but the desk is staffed twenty-four hours a day."

She nodded. "Thanks again."

"You're more than welcome."

I stepped away from the front desk and into the office behind. The one with no windows.

"Cover for me, Steve?" I asked. "I've gotta lock up before I wolf out. Moon's up in less than a minute."

Steve, the vampire, aimed a pair of finger guns at me and nodded. "Alright, Alex. See ya next week."

I nodded as I opened the door to my kennel. "Next week," I murmured through a mouth of teeth too large for my jaw.

Originally published in *Five Minutes at Hotel Stormcove*, May 2019.

Hashtag TPE

The Miskatonic University campus tour guides had a running betting pool: who would be the first to garner a TPE—or total prospect enrollment. They went so far as building up a hashtag (#tpe) for that mythical day, but getting an entire group of unruly high schoolers to complete the tour and sign their letters of intent was really nothing more than a fantasy.

Anthea Morrison had the lowest odds out of the whole bunch. Her first three campus tours had instead been "TPKs"—*none* of the touring seniors having made it through the whole tour. The normal attrition rate was around 25 percent, and the other student guides had started a side pool for how long it would be until the dean called Anthea in for dismissal from the guide program if not the university altogether. At least, that's what Naomi Carter claimed. None of the other students would confirm it, but Anthea saw the way they looked at her when they thought she wasn't looking. Pity from some, wonder at how she'd even made it into MiskU from others.

It wasn't that anyone expected her to keep all of the prospects interested. MiskU wasn't for everyone, after all. But Anthea was on a mission now. She wanted to prove all the other student tour guides wrong and be the first to bring back a TPE.

A stack of files lurked in her inbox. She pulled them out with some trepidation, noticing that three of the five had gold stars affixed to the front—high-priority students. In a way, that might make today's tour easier. Many of the high-priority students *wanted* to sign their MiskU enrollment intent letter the day they toured, so they were less likely to run screaming. But it also meant that any of those three who didn't complete the tour or sign at the end would reflect even more poorly on her record.

Anthea flipped through the files to get a sense of the students. *Tabitha Flynn, pre-med. Shiloh Cavanah, archaeology. Zeb Rutherford, folklore. Philip Darby, languages. Belladonna Whateley, library studies.*

The last one gave her pause both for the name and the intended major. Everyone in the area knew about the Whateley family. They'd been in the Miskatonic Valley for generations. And library studies meant taking the tour to the library, which was low on her list of places that led to a successful tour. Even regular MiskU students got lost in the book stacks on a weekly basis. She'd have to keep a close eye on her charges when they checked it out.

~

At admissions, a group of students and parents lingered in the lobby. Anthea gave them all a once-over. The two guys were as average white boy as average white boys could be while the girls appeared anything but. One of the girls looked Chinese, and Anthea pegged her as Tabitha but immediately chided herself for assuming the Chinese girl was the pre-med student. The second girl had ebony skin in dramatic contrast to the third girl, an albino.

Anthea put on her best chipper smile, hoping it would come through her voice as well. "Hi, everyone! I'm Anthea Morrison, and I'll be your tour guide this afternoon. I'll show you around the campus, and we'll make sure to stop off at all of the locations important to your prospective majors, and then we'll meet back up with your parents here so that you can sign your letters of intent if you so choose. I've got nametags for everyone—" She named each of the students, and they came forward to claim their nametags. She still couldn't differentiate between the boys aside from them wearing nametags now. The Chinese girl turned out to be Shiloh, while the Black girl was Tabitha, and the albino girl was Belladonna Whateley.

The woman beside the albino girl narrowed her eyes at Anthea. "I'm gonna go on the tour too."

Anthea forced her smile to broaden. "I'm sorry, ma'am, but we've found that the prospective students get a better sense of the school if they tour it without their family members. I understand that the admissions staff have some excellent refreshments for you here while you wait."

"I ain't drinkin' their Kool-Aid," Mrs. Whateley grumbled.

Ignoring her, Anthea smiled at the prospective students. "Shall we?"

The five high schoolers trailed behind Anthea, the guys bringing up the rear with Belladonna in front of them and Tabitha and Shiloh walking to either side of Anthea.

"So what do you major in?" Shiloh asked.

"Ancient history," Anthea replied. "There's a little bit of overlap with archaeology actually. Mostly on the anthropology side of things."

Shiloh nodded. "Do the ancient history students get to go on digs as well?"

"Ah, not really," Anthea said. "We're more inclined to see what the archaeology students have found and see if that fits into what we're researching."

"I am looking forward to the digs," Shiloh said, nodding for emphasis. "So many secrets hidden below the dirt."

"That there are," Anthea said, turning to walk backwards and face all of the students. "So how much do you all know about the history of Miskatonic University?"

"Founded forever ago and always dedicated to cutting-edge research and innovation while still honoring the past," Belladonna replied, her voice completely without inflection.

Anthea nodded. "Got it in one. Many of the buildings on this part of the campus are the original university buildings. They've been updated on the inside, but this part of campus looks just like it would have 'forever ago,' like Belladonna said. Conveniently, we've got one stop to make for those of you who plan to major in folklore, languages, and archaeology." Anthea gestured at one of the old stone buildings, which looked like it was held together solely by the ivy that covered it on all sides. Only a few of the windows had been cleared, and even they looked as though the ivy might overtake them as the campus slept. "This is also where most of my ancient history classes are held. It's sort of a catch-all for a lot of the history- and language-based majors."

Leading the group up the steps, Anthea continued. "There's a beginning-level Latin class that we can pop into for a moment if you'd like. Just about everyone takes at least a year of Latin because it's applicable to so many different subjects."

The door to the Latin classroom was open, and from within, they could hear the intonations of the class reciting what Anthea could identify as a verb declension. But she wasn't sure what verb it was, which puzzled her. She'd aced both semesters of Latin.

Peeking into the room, it became clear why the verb sounded so unfamiliar. This was the section of Latin for religious studies students, and based on the arrangement of the desks around the pentacle in the center of the floor, it looked like this was an exorcism not a verb declension.

Anthea scanned the room for the professor and realized the professor was the subject of the exorcism. He looked confused and a little terrified, and Anthea turned to herd the prospective students away from the open doorway. "You know what, wrong classroom."

"No, that's definitely Latin," Philip said, peering over Anthea's shoulder. "Fifth-century text, I'm pretty sure."

Cold sweat broke out all over Anthea's skin. This was how campus tours went sideways. If one of the prospective students decided to go into the classroom and somehow got involved with the exorcism, either they or another student wouldn't finish the tour. Through clenched teeth, Anthea said, "Well recognized. But it looks like they've got it all under control, so let's not get in their way. Oh hey, Belladonna, could you open that door?"

Belladonna looked between Anthea and the door and finally let out an exasperated sigh. "What, you mean with my hands?"

"Uh, yeah," Anthea said. "That's usually how doors work."

Belladonna shrugged but did as Anthea had requested.

The scene inside the other classroom was much more sedate with one student reading from a standard Latin textbook rather than an ancient tome. The professor nodded at Anthea, her eyes sparkling. As the student completed his reading, the professor said, "Class, it looks like we've got some prospective MiskU students in our midst. What do you say we give them a warm welcome in Latin?"

"Salvete omnes vos esse," the class intoned as one.

"Et salvete omnes vos esse," Anthea replied. "Thanks, Doctor Moore. We'll get out of your hair now." Anthea herded the touring students back into the hallway and closed the door to Doctor Moore's classroom.

Across the hall, the doorway to the religious studies Latin class was strobing between black and blood red, and a low-pitched squeal emanated from the room.

"Right," Anthea said. "Unfortunately, there aren't any folklore classes we can drop in on this afternoon, and I understand that most of the archaeology students are either in the field or the lab today. So let's head downstairs to see the labs."

"I think something's gone wrong with their ritual," Philip said, peering into the scintillating doorway.

"Well, we've got campus security for just that reason. So we don't need to worry about it," Anthea said.

"Yeah, but I might know how to fix it."

"As admirable as that is, seriously, you don't need to get involved." Anthea gestured to a phone receiver a few feet down the hallway. "You can make a report over there if it'll make you feel better."

Philip sighed but nodded, approaching the phone.

Anthea turned to herd the other students toward the stairs to the labs. "Ironically, our archaeology labs are all subterranean. So we're pulling things out of the dirt only to put them back underground."

Shiloh chuckled softly. "Very good."

"Hey, isn't he supposed to come with us?" Belladonna asked, pointing back the way they had come.

Anthea looked back just in time to see Philip leaping through the doorway into the Latin for Religious Studies classroom. *Dammit. No TPE today. At least he's not high priority.* Smiling at the group, she said, "Okay, well, hopefully he'll catch up to us downstairs."

As the high schoolers headed into the stairwell, Anthea glanced back toward the classroom. The doorway was now pitch black, and either fog or smoke had begun to roll out from it. She scribbled the classroom number on the palm of her hand in the hopes that she could send someone back to at least collect whatever was left of Philip Darby.

The hallway leading to the archaeology labs had long had wiring issues, and the lights flickered as they walked. "Most of what we'll see down here is what a lot of people consider the boring parts of archaeology. All of the artifacts that come in have to be cleaned, weighed, photographed, and cataloged. But there are some students who prefer that to field work, so there are two primary foci you can take with an archaeology major—field or lab studies." Anthea paused and knocked on one of the lab doors. The cataloging room seemed the safest bet to take her remaining four students into.

When no response came, Anthea tried the knob. The door opened with an eerie creak and revealed a room containing a dozen vacant computer stations.

"Where is everyone?" Zeb asked, wrinkling his nose at the empty room.

"This way," Shiloh said, pointing toward an open doorway to one side of the lab. The other students nudged past Anthea to follow Shiloh, and Anthea followed in their wake, unconsciously crossing her fingers.

"You know that doesn't work," Zeb said, glancing at Anthea's hands.

"Has that ever been proven?" Anthea shot back. She wondered, not for the first time, if it was too late in the year to get assigned to a different work study program.

Shiloh crouched on the floor near one of the lab tables. "Something fell and shattered," she said, reaching for a fragment of what looked like pottery.

"No, don't!" Anthea shouted. The students looked at her, and she said, much more calmly, "Proper lab protocol says that you should wear goggles and gloves at all times in the archaeology lab." She pointed toward a sign on the wall that said just that.

Shiloh rose and nodded. "Of course. Where would I find the proper safety equipment?"

Anthea pretended to look around the lab and shrugged. "You know what, I'm not really sure. But it looks like this area may have been evacuated. We might want to consider doing the same."

The students other than Shiloh shuffled out of the room, but Shiloh took her time looking around. "This looks like a good lab. I think—" Her voice cut off as her shoe brushed a fragment of the artifact, and she vanished.

"Okay, everyone watch where you step," Anthea said, her voice an octave higher than normal. "Don't touch anything, and just tiptoe until you're clear of this room." She scanned the floor before each step as she hurried toward the computer room and back into the hallway.

"Hey, is it cool if I just head back to admissions?" Zeb asked, his face now white as a sheet.

"You know what, that sounds like a great idea all around," Anthea replied. "Let's all go back to admissions."

Both Tabitha and Belladonna crossed their arms over their respective chests and shook their heads.

"I'm here to see the library," Belladonna said.

"And I the med school," Tabitha said.

"And I'm not going back to admissions until I've done so." Belladonna stamped her foot for emphasis like a spoiled three-year-old.

Anthea took a deep breath and let it out slowly. "Okay, alright. Let's walk Zeb back to the admissions building, and then we'll continue on the rest of the tour."

Zeb rolled his eyes. "Oh, come on. I'm not a baby. I can find my way back there on my own."

The lights in the hallway flickered out, leaving them in pitch darkness. Even the emergency exit lights seemed to have been snuffed out. All around, the sounds of shuffling feet echoed as if the entire hallway was filled with students.

When the lights flickered back on, Zeb was gone.

I've still got 40 percent. Anthea breathed deeply, trying to maintain her composure. She looked between Tabitha and Anthea and pulled a quarter from her pocket. "Heads we hit the med school next, tails we go see the library next."

The girls nodded, and Anthea flipped the coin. She slapped it down on her wrist and lifted her hand, and it showed heads. *Great.* "Alright, the West Building it is."

Tabitha and Belladonna both stuck close to Anthea as they made their way between the buildings. Overhead, the previously sunny day had turned overcast, the clouds with a weird purple tint to them.

"You often get weird weather like this here?" Tabitha asked.

"Mostly on Thursdays," Anthea said. "Or if the meteorology students are conducting experiments."

A bolt of lightning shot out from the clouds and struck the West Building ahead of them.

"Aw, crap," Anthea said. "Or if some med student thinks he's the next Victor Frankenstein." She turned to Tabitha. "So there it is, the West Building. I'm gonna guess it's about to go into containment, which means no one in or out until it's dealt with."

Tabitha sighed. "But I want to specialize in containment! This would be a fantastic opportunity for me to see exactly what that entails."

An iron portcullis slid down in front of the main entrance to the West Building, and Anthea pointed at it. "Sorry, Tabitha. We can't get in."

Tabitha pointed toward a unit of campus security officers jogging toward the building. "Are they going in?"

"Probably not. They're probably going to maintain a perimeter until they get word of what's actually happened." Anthea sighed. "I mean, it's like in the archaeology lab. There are a lot of rules, and you have to learn them and follow them if you want to be a student as MiskU. Rule one: if there's trouble, run the opposite direction. That's how you survive."

Tabitha grinned. "My rule one is to help. If it makes you feel better, I'll head to admissions as soon as I'm done and sign my letter."

"I appreciate that," Anthea said. "But I'd really feel better about this if you'd come with us to the library."

"Noted and rejected," Tabitha said. "You don't have to worry about me. I signed the waiver."

"C'mon," Belladonna said, tugging at Anthea's arm with fingers so cold she could feel them through her hoodie. "Let her go play hero if that's what she wants to do."

"Alright," Anthea said with a deep sigh. "Just remember. Running away from the problem is still an option. There are trained professionals here. You've got to survive if you ever want to become one of them."

Belladonna skipped away in the direction of the library while Anthea followed at a slower pace. She was well on her way to having no students with her when she got back to admissions. Even if Tabitha did survive to sign her letter of intent, Anthea was beginning to think that getting a TPE was just a dream, and the only thing that kept her going was the possibility that Naomi Carter would remain just as stymied as Anthea was in her pursuit of the lofty goal. Maybe it was time to drop the competitive streak and get a job in food services. At least the students there just got glassy-eyed and numb. That seemed easier.

"Hurry up, slowpoke," Belladonna called back, mirth evident in her voice for the first time since the tour had begun. She stopped and turned to look at Anthea. "You look miserable. Is it really that bad here?"

Anthea shook her head. "It's not all bad. There's good stuff too. I'm just doing a difficult job, and I'm not very good at it."

Belladonna frowned. "You're doing a fine job. We've seen a bunch of buildings, and now we're going to the library. Do you know how long I've waited to get into the library?"

"But the goal of my job is to get students to sign their letters of intent. Instead, I keep losing students." Anthea shrugged. "It's hard for them to enroll if they're not here."

"What makes you think they aren't here?" Belladonna asked.

Anthea looked at the girl, frowning. "What makes you think they are?"

"Philip and Zeb made it back to admissions. Shiloh teleported straight there from the lab. Tabitha will probably be fine since she's with campus security. They'll likely even walk her back to admissions afterward."

"Okay, wait. How do you know that Philip and Zeb and Shiloh all made it back to admissions?"

"Telepathy, duh."

Anthea sighed. "My current run of luck tells me you're full of it."

"Nah. My mom's side has loads of psychic abilities. Till her at least. Don't sweat it, okay? I get that you want to be good at your job, but maybe you just haven't met the right students until today. MiskU isn't for everyone, right?"

Anthea chuckled. "That's true." She sighed. "So you're dead set on the library?"

Belladonna shrugged. "I could wait a few more months if it helps. I'm going to enroll regardless. I just really want to see the library."

"Somehow, I think you'd do better there than a lot of people, Belladonna," Anthea said. "But your intuition's got me really curious. Tell you what. We'll go back to admissions and see who's there. And then if you still want to, I'll take you by the library."

"Can you come up with an excuse why my mom can't come with us?"

"It's restricted to current and future MiskU students? No general public allowed?"

"That'll work," Belladonna said, spitting into her palm and offering it to Anthea. "Deal."

Wincing, Anthea spit into her own palm and shook with Belladonna. "Deal."

~

Back at the admissions office, everything was as Belladonna had promised. Philip had helped stop the exorcism gone wrong and came back to admissions to sign his letter of intent. Shiloh had in fact teleported to the place she most wanted to be—the admissions office with pen in hand. Zeb had taken advantage of the blackout to duck the remainder of the tour, and he'd already enrolled for an independent study on the effects of crossed fingers on reality. And Tabitha had come back from the West Building to verify that it had indeed been a Victor Frankenstein–wannabe gone wrong but that the lightning bolt hadn't been enough to awaken his creature. So that crisis, too, had been averted. And she'd made good contacts with the containment force that she hoped to work with, and they had, just as Belladonna had suggested, accompanied her back to the admissions building.

Belladonna Whateley smiled at Anthea as she signed her letter. "You wanna get a picture of all five of us signing?" She frowned. "You're thinking something about a hashtag *T-P-E*?"

Anthea whipped out her phone. "Belladonna, you're kinda creepy, and I'd rather you not try to read my thoughts. But yeah. Hashtag *T-P-E*."

———

Originally published in *It Came from Miskatonic University*, July 2019.

About the Author

Dawn Vogel's academic background is in history, so it's not surprising that much of her fiction is set in earlier times. By day, she edits reports for historians and archaeologists. In her alleged spare time, she runs a craft business, co-runs a small press, and tries to find time for writing. Her steampunk adventure series, *Brass and Glass*, is available from DefCon One Publishing. She is a member of Broad Universe, SFWA, and Codex Writers. She lives in Seattle with her husband, author Jeremy Zimmerman, and their herd of cats.

Visit her at http://historythatneverwas.com.